A Nose for Trouble

TO YOSHA, EUBIE, AND YINNY

Library of Congress Cataloging in Publication Data
Singer, Marilyn.
A nose for trouble.
Summary: Canine detective Samantha Spayed helps her master
investigate industrial espionage at La Maison de Beauté, a women's
cosmetics company.
1. Children's stories, American. [1. Dogs—Fiction. 2. Mystery and
detective stories] I. Glass, Andrew, ill. II. Title.
PZ7.S6172Nos 1985 [Fic] 84-19761
ISBN: 0-03-001329-1

Designed by Susan Hood
Printed in the United States of America
1 2 3 4 5 6 7 8 9 10

ISBN 0-03-001329-1

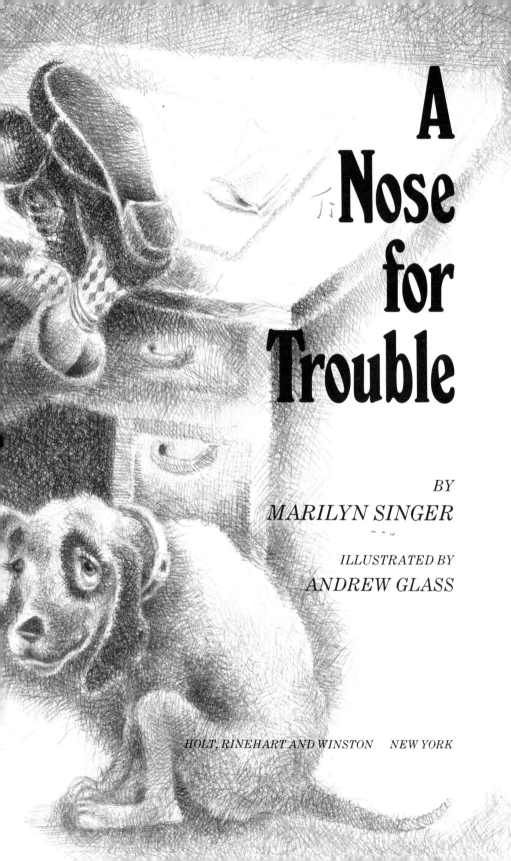

A Nose for Trouble

BY

MARILYN SINGER

ILLUSTRATED BY

ANDREW GLASS

HOLT, RINEHART AND WINSTON   NEW YORK

A Nose for Trouble

CHAPTER
—1—

She was small, blonde, and very confused. I could tell that before she opened her mouth. But just how confused was a surprise even to me, and it takes a lot to surprise Samantha Spayed.

I should've known it was going to be one of those days even before the confused blonde showed up. All afternoon I'd had an itch on my nose. That itch always means trouble.

Besides my itchy nose, there was Barlowe working on those slogans again. Whenever we get broke enough, Barlowe starts entering contests. He's always hoping to win big bucks. The only thing he's won so far is thanks from the post office for shelling out so much dough on stamps.

A word about Barlowe, in case his name doesn't ring a bell, which it should because he's been in the papers a lot. Philip Barlowe's a detective. They say he solved a lot of cases, including *The Fido Frame-Up*. But if you were smart enough to read my account of the story, you'd know who really did the job. That's right—yours truly.

After *The Fido Frame-Up*, I decided that I was going to sit back and let Barlowe try to solve our next case by himself. I was tired of not getting any credit. I promised myself I'd hang around as a bodyguard just in case things got sticky, but otherwise I'd take it easy. The problem is I figured we'd be on another case right away. I didn't guess we'd both be taking it easy for so long. For two long months nobody banged on our door except the landlord. Nobody called us at odd hours. And nobody'd given us any money. Hence, Barlowe's contest binge. What contest he was entering this time I didn't know, and I didn't want to know.

But Barlowe told me anyway. "What do you think of this, Sam? 'Elegant ladies used Eggelant (Egg-Rich) Shampoos.' Nah. How about this one: 'Eggelant (Egg-Rich) Shampoo is no yolk.' Ha-ha. Get it?"

I wondered if Barlowe used the stuff himself and it had scrambled his brains. I left him laughing to himself and went to the kitchen for some chow—lousy, cheap stuff, but better than nothing. Just then, the buzzer rang. I immediately went into my watchdog act.

"Who is it?" Barlowe asked through the intercom.

"Me. Roper," a voice answered.

I stopped the watchdog number. Barlowe didn't need protection from Mandy Roper. She's a pal, a zookeeper and, in Barlowe's own words, "one swell dame." Roper hadn't been around in a while. She took a trip to Europe and sent us a couple of postcards. She'd wanted Barlowe and me to go with her, but he'd turned her down. He'd said we needed a rest, and that traipsing around Europe wouldn't be one. I wouldn't have minded going alone with her, but nobody'd asked me. Roper was hurt that Barlowe refused. She didn't say she was, but I could tell. Noticing things like that is part of my job.

When Barlowe opened the door for Roper, I gave her the Big Greeting. I jumped up and down, licked her hands and face, barked happily, the whole bit. I only do the Big Greeting for a couple of people, and Roper, knowing that, had the good sense to be flattered. "Whoa, whoa, Sam, old buddy. It's good to see you, too," she said.

Barlowe was cooler than me. "Hello, Mandy," he said.

"Hello, Phil."

"Have a good trip?"

"Very good. How's work been?"

"It hasn't."

There they were, two old friends acting like near strangers. Then, Barlowe said, "I missed you, Mandy."

"I missed you too, Phil."

They hugged each other. I gave them a small *woof* of encouragement.

They broke apart and Roper handed Barlowe a pile of envelopes and said gruffly, "Don't you ever collect your mail? The postman said he couldn't fit any more stuff in your box."

"Who needs a bunch of bills?" Barlowe said.

An envelope slid to the floor. I gave it a sniff. There was something familiar about the smell. Familiar and delicious. One thing I knew, it wasn't a bill. I picked it up with my teeth and nudged Barlowe's leg. My nose was itching like crazy, but I tried to ignore it.

Barlowe took the envelope. "What's this? La Maison de Beauté? Never heard of them. I sure don't owe them any money."

I'd never heard of them either, but I liked that smell, so I nudged him harder. Roper took the envelope from him. "La Maison de Beauté. They make cosmetics. I use their bath oil. It's good stuff." She opened the envelope, took out a single sheet of paper, and read:

"Dear Mr. Barlowe,

"Word of your talent and discretion in solving cases has reached me via a mutual acquaintance, Lady Binghampton-Nuggets. I require your assistance in a matter both urgent and delicate. Please come to my office at 560 Garson Boulevard on Tuesday, June 4, at 5:30 P.M. If you cannot make it, then call me at 555-1357.

"Thank you.

Sincerely,
Roger de France
President"

Tuesday, June 4, at 5:30! I let out a howl. I could almost smell real meat again.

"What's eating you, Sam?" Barlowe asked.

"Barlowe, do you know what day this is?" Roper asked.

"Yeah, Tuesday."

"Which Tuesday?"

"June fourth."

"Right. And what time is it, Barlowe?"

He looked at his watch. "Five-fifteen."

"Five-sixteen to be exact," Roper said, looking at her own. "It takes twenty minutes to get to Garson Boulevard. If you leave right now you'll be only six minutes late."

I howled in agreement. I'd said I'd stay out of Barlowe's next case. But there at least had to be a case for me to stay out of.

"Five-thirty. I have another appointment at five-thirty."

I knew about Barlowe's "other appointment." It was at Rex King's Bar. I picked up a hard rubber bone some relative of Barlowe's bought for me for Christmas, and which Barlowe used as a doorstop, and pitched it at him. It hit his shin.

"Owww. Take it easy, Sam. Okay, okay. I'll postpone my other five-thirty appointment. Let's go."

Thinking about porterhouse steak, I bounded out the door ahead of him.

On the drive to La Maison de Beauté, Barlowe kept working on his slogans. And I kept my head out the window so I didn't have to hear him. We were just approaching Garson Boulevard when he stopped the clunker of a Buick dead in the middle of the street (at least, I hoped he'd stopped it; The Clunker, as I called it, which we bought with the money from the last case, has been known to die by itself at the worst possible moments). I fell back onto the seat. "I've got it!" Barlowe yelled. "Sam, you'll love this one. Here it is: 'A man's best friend is his dog, but a woman's best friend is her Egg-elant (Egg-Rich) Shampoo.' Isn't that great . . ."

I didn't hear the rest of what he said because just then the blonde staggered into view. And coming at her from the other direction was a big, black sedan.

"*Whoo!*" I howled, meaning, Watch out! I leaped out the

4

open window and heard Barlowe yell, "Hey!" The black sedan screeched to a halt, and the car behind it smashed into its fender. I dashed up to the blonde.

"Come on. Follow me," I said.

She didn't seem to hear.

"Come on!" I ordered.

She gave me a blank look, but she followed me, weaving in and out of traffic that had piled up on Garson Boulevard.

We reached the Clunker. Barlowe opened the door. "Sam, are you okay? You could've been hurt."

I gave him a quick *woof* to let him know I was fine. Then we both looked at the blonde. She was hobbling a little, but there wasn't a scratch on her.

Barlowe opened the back door. The blonde stumbled onto the seat.

I scrambled up behind her.

"What's your name? Your address?" I asked.

She gave me that same blank stare. Then she opened her mouth and said, "Yoghurt."

I stared at her, and then it hit me. The blonde was more than confused. The blonde had amnesia. No good-looking, self-respecting blonde cocker spaniel would let herself be called Yoghurt.

CHAPTER
—2—

The spaniel stayed in the car while Barlowe and I crossed the wide parking lot to La Maison de Beauté. The place looked like one of those fancy haciendas they've got in Southern California, where Barlowe and I once went on vacation. Why anyone would build a makeup factory with a French name to look like an old Spanish house was one mystery I don't feel like solving. There were even potted palm trees next to the entrance. I gave them a sniff. Plastic.

Barlowe rang the bell next to the door. Waiting for someone to answer, he said to me, "I didn't notice any tags on that dog, Sam. But we'll have to stop at the pound and see if anyone reported her."

At the mention of the pound, I felt my hairs prickle. I'd spent a night there not so long ago and going back there any time soon was just *too* soon for me.

Nobody came to the door, so Barlowe rang the bell a second time. "We'll also call the cops and check the papers," he went on. "Jeez, isn't anybody home here?"

Casually, I leaned against the door. It opened.

"Hey, it's open," Barlowe said, following me in.

One of Barlowe's biggest talents is telling you what you already know.

We made our way to the front desk. The receptionist was fumbling under it and muttering, "Darn that pencil."

"Ahem." Barlowe cleared his throat.

"Be right with ya," she said. "Here it is." She raised her head.

I stayed put, but Barlowe must've set the world record for the backward long jump. Except for her eyes, the receptionist's face was completely covered with some thick, light-colored goo with an interesting smell. On her head was a shower cap. She looked worse than Barlowe did when he went to Roper's last Halloween party dressed as a zombie.

"Oh my, sorry I scared you. I forgot how I look."

If I looked like that, I'd want to forget it too, I thought.

"I'm trying out a new product for Mr. de France," she explained.

I began to edge a little closer to the desk. The smell was more interesting than I thought. It was delicious. Just like the envelope de France's letter had come in.

"Aren't you afraid of scaring away customers?" Barlowe asked.

"We don't get customers here—just salespeople and staff. You're our last visitor for the day. Who are you, anyway?"

"The name's Barlowe. Philip Barlowe. And this is Samantha Spayed. We have an appointment with Mr. de France."

"I'm Allison Keys, and I see you do, right here in the book. Go down that corridor and turn left and you'll see Mr. de France's office."

"Come on, Sam," Barlowe called.

But the goo was exerting such a powerful influence over me I did something I never would have done otherwise. Without thinking, I jumped onto the receptionist's lap and began licking her face.

"Sam!" Barlowe yelled.

"Friendly, isn't she?" said the receptionist, giggling and trying to push me off.

Suddenly, I came back to my senses. I was giving the Big Greeting to a total stranger. Mortified, I slid off and slunk down the hall behind Barlowe, who apologized for my behavior. I'd just learned what it felt like to make a fool of myself—and I vowed then and there never to do it again.

We found de France's office without any trouble. De France was a skinny little guy with a big nose and a thin moustache who looked like he'd be more at home serving omelettes than sitting behind a big desk. His French accent was so thick you could spread it on bread—but to me it sounded more like margarine than butter.

"Ah, Meester Bahrrrlowe," he said, "I am 'appy to meet you. You are famous on boz sides of ze ocean."

"Yeah," said Barlowe. "Let's get down to business."

De France clapped his hands. "Ah, I like a man who knows 'is own mind. Business, as you put it, is zis." From the top drawer of his desk he took out a small jar. "Zis is our new product—a skin *crème* called Crème de Beauté wiz Secret Formula 36. It is a wonderful product. Very French. Ze French know all ze secrets of *beauty*." He pronounced it *bow-tay*. "And I should know zey do. I am born and raised in Paree."

Barlowe stifled a yawn. I didn't bother to stifle mine.

"Anyway, to get back to ze problem. Ze secret formula is locked in a vault to which only I 'ave ze combination."

"I thought you said the secret formula's in the cream," Barlowe said.

Oh brother, I thought. If you ever want to get out of the detective business, Barlowe, you could apply for a job as straight man in a comedy team.

"I mean ze composition of ze formula is in a vault."

"The composition?"

De France was beginning to lose his temper. "Ze list of stuff and 'ow it is put together. Ze recipe. Ze works."

"Oh, I get it," said Barlowe. "The recipe's locked in the vault."

"Right."

"You're afraid someone wants to steal it."

De France's eyes bugged out. " 'Ow did you know zat?"

"Simple. Why would you bother to lock something up in a vault if you weren't afraid of its being stolen?"

De France recovered his composure. "Why, Meester Bahrrrlowe, you are ze most cleverest man. You are eggzactally right. I am afraid of someone stealing zis formula. And I weel tell you who zat someone is."

My ears perked up. Barlowe will never even miss my help, I thought. This character is going to hand him a solved case before he lifts a finger.

"Who?" asked Barlowe.

"Barry Slick, zat's who."

"Barry Slick? Who's he?"

" 'E is ze president of Ze 'Ouse of Good Looks and my arch rival. A terrible . . . 'ow you say . . . slimy leetle man—except 'e is not leetle. 'E weel try to steal ze formula and come out wiz 'is own skin *crème* before La Maison de Beauté does. 'E 'as done zat two times before—once 'e stole a *parfum* and ze second time a 'air conditioner."

"An air conditioner? Right out of your office?"

"Not my office."

"And no one saw him do it? An air conditioner's a big thing."

Oh brother! I thought again and wished I could put my paws over my ears.

"Mon Dieu!" exclaimed de France, slapping his forehead. "A 'air conditioner. 'Air. Like on ze 'ead."

"Oh, I get it," said Barlowe for the second time in less than five minutes. "A *hair* conditioner."

De France sighed with relief.

"So you want me to make sure Slick doesn't steal your new skin *crème*, er, cream this time."

De France looked like he was about to kiss Barlowe on both cheeks. "So smart 'e is. *Oui*, I do. If 'e steal it, it cost me 'undreds of zousands of dollars in advertising and sales. But zere is more."

Aha. I thought this case sounded too easy.

9

"Ze only way Slick could 'ave gotten ze last two formulas is if someone in *my* company leaked ze information to 'im. I want you to find out who zat is and stop 'im or 'er."

"Who has access to the information?" asked Barlowe.

"Only ze *trois* chemists who worked on ze formula: Paul Swete, Amy Darling, and Bunson Burner. And me, of course."

"Any guesses which one it is?" asked Barlowe.

De France shook his head. "I 'ate to zink it is any of zem. But zere is no one else it could be."

Just then, the door opened, and a woman who looked like she could lift de France with one finger clattered in. She had a big nose like de France's, and a raggy kerchief was wrapped around her head. She was carrying a mop and a pail. The minute I smelled her, I sneezed. Ammonia. It always does it to me. She set down the pail with a *thump*. "Hey, you still here?" she boomed in a voice as large as her frame. "I gotta get my work done."

"Oh, I am so, so sorry, Sadie. We weel be done soon," said de France. He looked scared to death of her. And I wondered why.

Sadie gave him a look that reminded me of a bad-tempered boxer I once knew. "All right. I'll start in the lab. But you better be finished soon."

"I promise," he answered.

Sadie clattered back out.

De France looked apologetic. "Good 'elp is 'ard to find. And she is very . . . er . . . efficient," de France said. He turned to an open window and took a deep breath.

"I'd like to interview those chemists today," Barlowe said.

"I'm afraid you can't," said de France, sounding calm once again.

"Why?"

"Bunson Burner and Amy Darling have left for ze day. And zere goes Paul Swete now." He pointed out the window.

Barlowe and I trotted over and looked out. A young man was skipping toward the parking lot. He was whistling a jaunty tune.

10

"Ah, zere goes a man in love. We French know about *l'amour*," said de France.

I hoped he wasn't about to break into a cancan. Fortunately, he remembered what we were here for. "You can talk to all of zem tomorrow," he said.

"We'll do that, Mr. de France," said Barlowe.

"One more zing, Meester Bahrrrlowe. I 'ave already told ze people 'ere I intend to 'ire you. To maybe put zem off leaking, *si vous comprenez* . . . er . . . if you comprehend."

"I see," said Barlowe. "No undercover stuff then."

"Ah, not quite. I also told zem I am 'iring a new chemist. You must 'ave an *operative* you work wiz." De France smiled, obviously proud he knew the word.

Unlike Barlowe. "Huh?" he said.

De France didn't hear him. "Good," he said. "Then you can get your operative to pose as ze chemist."

Barlowe's vocabulary got a sudden new addition. "Oh, an *operative*," he said.

De France looked at him strangely. "Don't you have one? I thought I was 'iring a pro. I could 'ave sent for Nero Wolfe—"

"Yeah, sure I've got an operative," said Barlowe quickly.

This time I gave him the strange look. In case you haven't been following all this, an operative is someone a detective hires to do a certain amount of footwork for him. It's perfectly legit and pretty common to hire one too. I've sort of got an operative I use. Name of Harry. But Barlowe doesn't. For one thing, he prefers to work alone. For another, he can't afford it. Operatives don't come cheap. Harry can tell you that. But even Barlowe must've realized how much we needed this case—or rather the dough from it.

"Good," said de France, sweetness and light once more. "Send 'im or 'er to me first and I'll set things up."

"Will do," said Barlowe.

"Oh, and Meester Bahrrrlowe, 'ere is a key to La Maison de Beauté, in case you need to come in when no one is 'ere."

"Thanks. Come on, Sam."

We left the office and headed down the hall. We decided to

take a brief tour of the building. It was pretty quiet, so the noises coming from a room at the end of the corridor sounded especially loud. I trotted over to the door and sniffed at it. I felt the hairs on my neck rise. Ammonia. This time mixed with some kind of perfume that smelled worse than Moonlight in Chicago, my least favorite scent. I knew I shouldn't tip off Barlowe after swearing I'd let him handle the case alone, but old habits die hard.

"We'll have to come back tomorrow, Sam. Looks like everyone's gone," Barlowe said.

I didn't want to make any noise, so I just stood there with my nose stuck out and my tail straight like a pointer pal of mine once taught me.

"Find something interesting, Sam?" Barlowe called loud enough for de France at the other end of the hall to hear. He came over and turned the doorknob.

"Hey!" a hefty voice bellowed. "You and that dog can't come in here. I'm cleaning."

Whew, I thought, with that scent, who wants to? I wondered why she'd bothered to put it on. I didn't think she had a date after work.

Sadie stomped over and pulled the door shut, but not before I got a glimpse of what she'd been doing before we opened it. She'd been picking over the contents of a wastepaper basket which she had spread all over a counter. I call that a funny way to clean.

"Well, let's call it a day, Sam. I'll interview the three suspects tomorrow."

As we headed for the exit, I heard a slight noise behind us. I turned my head and looked down the hall. Sadie was staring at us. When she saw me, she ducked back in the room. Well, Barlowe, I said to myself, you just missed your chance to interview suspect number four.

CHAPTER
—3—

The confused blonde was still in the same shape we'd left her in. "How are you feeling?" I asked her. She didn't answer.

Barlowe drove to the pound, muttering to himself all the way there, "Operative, operative, who's got an operative?" When he went in, I stayed in the car with the spaniel. Barlowe returned quickly. He looked at the spaniel and said, "Well, pretty lady, looks like no one's reported losing you." He patted her head. "We'll fix you up with some grub and then I'll try the cops. But first, time to keep that other appointment."

I knew what appointment that was. King's Bar. "Hope you don't find this joint too low-down," I said. I knew I was being nasty and that the spaniel hadn't done anything to deserve it. But the truth is I was feeling a little miffed at Barlowe's attention to her. He never called me pretty lady. I may not be as good-looking as the blonde, but I still have a certain appeal.

By the time we got to King's, I was feeling better. We were working again, and that meant I might get that juicy bit of porterhouse in the not too distant future. Then I remembered my resolution to let Barlowe handle the case himself and I wondered if, instead of steak, I'd soon be chomping on boiled shoe leather.

If the spaniel minded King's Bar, she didn't let on. She followed us in and sat quietly in a corner with me while Barlowe went to get a beer. I was trying to figure out a way to make conversation when a husky voice whispered in my ear, "How's tricks, Sam?"

I turned my head, "Not bad, Harry." He looked even scruffier than usual, but I was glad to see him. In this business, good operatives are hard to come by.

"You must be on a case," he said.

"Yeah."

"So, you gonna introduce me to your good-looking friend?"

I decided to be cagey. "Don't you recognize her?"

Harry scratched his ear. I backed away a little. I'd just gotten over the last case of fleas I got from him. "Can't say that I do. What's your name, sweetheart?"

The spaniel stared dully at him.

Harry looked at her and then at me. "Hey, is she—er—?"

"No. She's got amnesia."

"Amnesia! Whew!"

"Yeah, I was hoping you might know who she is—nobody reported her or anything."

"Well, I don't know her, but for a small fee—say a couple of burgers—"

"Forget it, Harry. I haven't finished paying you for the last case."

"I'll settle for franks—"

"I said forget it."

He stared at the spaniel again. "She sure is good-looking. She have anything to do with your new case?"

"Nothing, as far as I know."

"Tell you what. I'll be a sport and nose around a little for free."

Males sure get swayed by a pretty face, I thought. But I said, "Thanks, Harry. I appreciate it—and so will she."

"Don't you want to tell old Harry your name, sweetheart?"

"She told me it was Yoghurt," I said.

"No way," Harry said.

"That's what I thought."

We both looked at her.

She yawned and daintily licked her lips. "Beauty," she said.

"Beauty," said Harry. "Now, that's more like it."

She fluttered her eyes a little.

Oh brother! I thought, and began to wish I hadn't been so quick to jump out of the car to rescue her.

Roper was still there when we got back to the apartment. "Who's this?" she asked, stooping down for a better look at the spaniel.

Barlowe explained. The spaniel stared back at Roper and I watched her eyes lose that glazed look. She began to wag her tail. This is it, I thought. She's coming out of it. We'll find out who she is and get her home fast so I can have a good night's sleep. Then, before I could ask her a single question, her tail drooped and her eyes went blank just like before. Roper didn't seem to notice. "She's a real beauty," she said. "Look at that color. Feel that soft fur."

Oh no, not Roper too. What does Beauty or Yoghurt or whatever her name is have that I don't, besides amnesia?

I walked up to Roper and nudged her hand. "Hi, Sam," she said. But she kept on scratching the spaniel.

"I'll call the cops in a bit. If they don't know anything about the dog, I'll post an ad in the paper," Barlowe said.

Roper chucked the spaniel under the chin. "Very calm, isn't she?" Then she said to Barlowe, "So, how did it go?"

"Okay," he answered.

"Just okay? Listen, Barlowe, don't play the close-mouthed detective with me. I know you better than that. What's the scoop?"

"There isn't any." Barlowe began checking his fingernails as if the solution to the case was under them.

"Well, listen. If you need any help on this one, let me know."

Barlowe's head shot up. "What makes you think I need any help?"

"Because you're dealing with women's *cosmetics*, wise guy. A field I don't think you're too familiar with. And neither is Sam. Although she's got a couple of advantages you don't— her ears and her nose." She patted my head.

I began to feel a little better, even though she left out my major asset. My brain.

"Women's cosmetics, eh?" Barlowe rubbed his chin. "Roper, you wouldn't . . . er . . . know anything about . . . er . . . chemistry, would you?"

"I most certainly would. It was my minor in college."

Barlowe smiled his most charming smile. At least, he thinks it's charming. I think it makes him look like he's got gas pains.

"Mandy, how would you like a job?"

"I've got a job."

"For one week only . . . you've still got a week's vacation, don't you?"

Roper looked suspicious. "Does this job pay?"

"Sure."

She perked up.

"It pays you my undying gratitude."

She groaned. Then, she said, "All right. What is it?"

"I need someone with a background in chemistry to act as my operative at La Maison de Beauté and try to find out who might be leaking information to a rival company." He paused a moment. "Well, will you do it?"

"What, play both a chemist and a detective for a week? Are you nuts?"

Barlowe looked deflated. I admit I was too. I could see my steak sprout wings and fly away. So I did something I reserve for last-hope situations. I walked over and put my paw on Roper's knee and moaned.

She looked down at me and giggled. "You want me to do it too, Sam?"

"*Mmmmoofff*," I said mournfully.

She smiled a moment, then said, "All right."

"You will?" Barlowe almost shouted.

"I just said I would."

Barlowe threw his arms around her. I gave her the Big Greeting. Then Barlowe got embarrassed and dropped his arms.

"Now, you better give me all the details," Roper said.

He did. Then we celebrated with some ice cream Barlowe'd bought. I was feeling pretty good—until Roper looked at the spaniel again. "You know, if you don't find this sweetheart's owner, I might be interested in keeping her."

That did it. Roper, you traitor. I began to slink toward the closet I use when I need to be alone. But I got stopped by the ringing of the phone.

Now, the other thing Barlowe invested in besides the Buick when we got paid for *The Fido Frame-Up* is a nifty little gadget that lets you listen and talk into the phone from any part of the room. All you have to do is flick a switch. Barlowe said he got it so he could take notes more easily when he talked. I say he got it because he's lazy. He expects me to flick the switch while he just sits there. I didn't feel like obliging.

But Roper did. And that's how we all got to hear a hoarse voice that could have been male or female say, "Stay away from La Maison de Beauté."

"*Bbooof*," I said, meaning, Who is this?

Barlowe repeated my line.

"Just stay away," the voice said again, and the caller hung up.

"Whew! This case sure sounds like a hot one," said Roper.

"You sure you want to work on it?" Barlowe sounded worried, whether for himself or Roper I couldn't tell.

"I said I would. A little thing like that doesn't scare me. We get cranks all the time at the zoo." She patted the spaniel's head again.

This time, I didn't let it bother me. I was too busy wondering who could've made that call. I know a crank when I hear one, and that didn't sound like a crank to me.

CHAPTER
—4—

The air was balmy; the sky was clear; and all the dogs in the neighborhood were full of pep. Except for me—I was dog-tired. I'd spent the night fighting for space on my bed. The spaniel kept shoving me off it. She was having these dreams. She'd twitch and whine and kick her legs. And I'd end up on the floor. I kept hoping at least she'd say something that might turn out to be useful, but the only things that came out of her mouth were sounds, not words. So I got no sleep and no clues. In the morning, when it was time to leave, Barlowe had to call me twice before I picked myself up and staggered over to him. Now, you're probably wondering why I didn't just stay there and take it easy like I said I would. The truth is I didn't want to spend the day hanging out with the blonde.

But I was out of luck again. "Okay, pretty lady, you can come too," Barlowe called. The spaniel, looking blank as ever, ambled over. "Sam could use a little company."

I gave Barlowe a dirty look, but he didn't seem to notice.

The spaniel was quiet in the car. She didn't sleep, and she didn't talk either. I still didn't get any shut-eye because Barlowe was singing some corny old songs at the top of his lungs. What's he so happy about? I asked myself grumpily. Then, I realized he was feeling good because: (1) He was on a case again; (2) He'd mailed off his entry to the Eggelant contest that morning; and (3) He *had* had a good night's sleep.

I decided that tonight the spaniel was going to share *his* bed.

The blonde stayed in the Buick once again while we picked our way across La Maison de Beauté's parking lot. Because it was working hours, the lot was packed with cars. As I squeezed between two cars, I thought I heard a funny noise nearby. It was a high-pitched sound like a dog yapping. "Hello?" I said. Nobody answered. I shrugged, thinking someone had left a radio on somewhere, and forgot about it. I shouldn't have.

In the front office, Allison Keys, who looked like a pleasant, middle-aged woman without her monster makeup, gave us a big smile.

"Good morning, Mr. Barlowe. And Sam."

I did the tail-wagging bit. To tell you the truth, I was glad she wasn't angry at my previous embarrassing behavior.

"Mr. de France said you can visit the lab first today."

"Good," said Barlowe.

The receptionist rummaged in her desk and pulled out something. "Here's your pass," she said. And that's when I noticed her fingernails. They were about an inch long and so shiny they almost hurt my eyes. The day before they'd been short and dull. Now they looked like gleaming deadly weapons.

"Ouch," Barlowe said, reaching for the pass. One of her fingernails was stuck in his palm like an oversized splinter.

"Oh my, I'm so sorry," she said, grabbing a tweezer and pulling out the nail.

"Another new product?" growled Barlowe, sucking his wounded hand.

"Yes, I'm afraid so. Perma-Nails. I'll have to tell Mr. de France they're not working as well as he hoped."

"You can say that again," said Barlowe. "You can also tell

him I'll send him the bill for my tetanus shot." Grabbing the pass, he strode down the hall. I had to trot to keep up with him.

We went straight to the lab. Paul Swete was bending over a strange-looking arrangement of test tubes and beakers. His brow was furrowed with concentration.

But he looked up when we walked in. His brow cleared, and he broke into a sweet smile. "Hey, what a nice girl," he said, stooping to pet me.

Now, I don't usually let anybody call me girl. But, somehow, coming from Paul Swete it didn't sound so bad. I let him pat my head and scratch my ears.

Then he straightened up. "Mr. de France said to give you a quick tour of the lab. This is the communal lab. We run our experiments in here. We each have a cubicle with a desk in it. I'll walk you through so you get the layout."

He took us from one cubicle to another, pointing out who worked in each and scratching me behind the ears every so often. He seemed a little bit sad to me. But I didn't know why. I tried cheering him up by giving his hand a lick every now and then. I knew that wasn't professional conduct with a suspect, but I've got a soft spot for people who treat me with respect.

"This is Bunson Burner's room. He's in the library right now. Said he had to check up on an old formula. You can talk to him later. Over here's where Amy Darling works."

I heard a little catch in his voice when he said her name. And I knew right away that Swete had it bad for her. I also guessed his present sadness had something to do with her as well. I wondered where she was.

Barlowe was obviously wondering the same thing because he asked.

"She called in this morning and said her mother is sick and she had to leave town to take care of her. She didn't say when she'd be back," Swete said mournfully. "Allison, the receptionist, said Amy sounded kind of funny. Hardly like Amy at all, she said. I guess she's worried about her mother. I don't know why she didn't call me . . ." His voice trailed off.

I felt sorry for the guy. Sick mother excuses are as old as the hills. I think Barlowe felt sorry for him, too, because he gave Swete a little pat on the shoulder and changed the subject. "What about this next room? Whose is it?"

Swete gave himself a little shake and me a little scratch and told us, "This room's another lab for the new chemist who's coming today. It's got special equipment only an expert can use. It's been locked since the last chemist left."

I wondered why the last chemist had left, but Swete didn't say and Barlowe didn't ask.

We got to Swete's cubicle last. Then Barlowe said, "Thanks for the tour. Now I've got just a couple of questions to ask you."

"Sure," said Swete. "Ask away."

Barlowe sat down at Swete's desk and scanned the top of it. He picked up a framed photo and stared at it. "This Amy Darling?"

"That's her," said Swete, sounding like he was about to burst into song.

"She's a looker," said Barlowe. I might have guessed he'd get sidetracked by a pretty face. "She reminds me a little of Roper . . . um . . . of someone I know."

Swete smiled. "Yes?"

I yawned. It looked like Barlowe was going to spend the day chewing the fat. But then he set down the picture. "How long have you been working here?"

"Almost three years."

"What products have you worked on?"

"Lots. A couple of shampoos, several perfumes, a hair conditioner."

"And the latest skin cream?"

"Yes, that too—"

Just then, the phone rang. It was in a little glassed-in cubicle within the lab. "Excuse me," said Swete. I wanted to follow him, but he closed the door tight before I got there. So instead, I nosed around the lab, telling myself I wasn't really helping Barlowe, just fooling around. Hanging in the air was a faint familiar smell. The receptionist's goo, I realized, licking my lips. There were other smells too—some better than others, but nothing out of the ordinary. Barlowe shuffled through some of the papers on Swete's desk, but he didn't seem to discover anything unusual there, either.

We both heard the office door open and turned back to Swete. And it didn't take good eyes to realize something had happened to him. But Barlowe didn't seem to notice. "So Mr. Swete, about that skin cream . . ."

"I'm a busy man, Mr. Barlowe. I don't have any time to talk to you now," Swete said. One eyelid was twitching. He touched it with trembling fingers, then wiped the sweat from his top lip. I edged closer to him and took a good whiff. The smell I recognized was unmistakable. It was Fear. I was sorry to smell it. And even sorrier that Paul Swete suddenly had something to hide.

Swete brushed past me and went over to his desk. He picked a stray beaker off it.

"Just one more question," Barlowe persisted. "You know anything about the leaks of the formulas for some of these products you've been working on to Barry Slick's outfit?"

Crash! The beaker landed on the floor. Swete just stared at it. Then he seemed to calm down. Or maybe he just deflated. "I don't know anything about anything—except chemistry. I suggest you talk to Bunson Burner."

"Okay, Mr. Swete. Maybe you'll have more time to talk later."

Swete didn't answer. He just started to sweep up the broken glass.

Barlowe loped out of the room without asking Swete who'd phoned him, which wasn't too bright. I wondered how much longer I could hold out and let Barlowe bungle this one. I gave it anywhere from two hours to two minutes.

On the way to the library, we ran into Mr. de France, the

receptionist, and another woman. "Oh, Meester Bahrrrlowe," said de France. "I'd like you to meet our new chemist. Miss Keys is going to 'elp 'er get settled." He gave Barlowe a huge wink.

Barlowe and I stared at the chemist. She had her hair piled on top of her head, a pair of glasses perched on her nose, and a lab coat covering whatever else she was wearing. I had to admit she'd done a good job. Roper looked like a pro.

I didn't give any sign of recognition, but Barlowe wasn't so controlled. He started to laugh and had to fake a cough to cover it up.

Roper acted like nothing had happened. She extended her hand and said in a crisp voice, "Sandy Hoper."

Her name sent Barlowe into a fresh coughing fit. "Sorry . . . hay fever," he gasped. He managed to shake her hand.

Roper nodded. "If there's anything I can do for you, let me know. I'll be in the lab."

I have to admit, even I was impressed.

Barlowe finished coughing and we headed for the library.

Bunson Burner was standing by a bookshelf, his long nose buried in a large volume. He was copying something down and mumbling strange words to himself in a high-pitched voice that could've sounded like a man's or a woman's if you heard it over a speaker phone like the one we've got. "Lithospermum. Litzia . . ." he was saying.

Barlowe cleared his throat. "Mr. Burner?"

"Argggh," squeaked the chemist. He shoved the paper into the book, slammed it shut, and shoved it back on the shelf like it was hot. "H-how long h-have you b-been st-standing there?" he stammered. "W-who are y-you?"

"Philip Barlowe. And this is Sam Spayed."

Burner ran a hand over his bald head and started to laugh. "Oh, Mr. Barlowe, I'm sorry. I thought you were the new chemist Mr. de France is hiring. I haven't met him—or her—yet."

And it sure doesn't seem like you want to, I thought.

Burner rattled on, "I'm very pleased to meet you, Mr. Barlowe. I read about your last case and was very impressed. Clever how you caught those crooks."

I could see Barlowe's head swell. Which is probably why he didn't bother to ask why Burner would be happier to see a detective than a fellow chemist.

"Mr. de France said you'd be coming by to ask some questions about the new product," Burner continued. "What do you want to know?"

Barlowe sat down in a chair. "I want to know how you, Paul Swete, and Amy Darling came up with the skin cream. Do you always work as a team?"

"Not always. We sometimes work alone. But we have worked together a lot. A couple of times Sol Ubal worked with us too."

"Sol Ubal? Who's he?"

That's what I wanted to know.

"Another chemist. He quit a couple of weeks ago to work for The House of Good Looks."

"Barry Slick's outfit?"

Burner made a face. "Yes."

A chemist who went to work for Barry Slick. The suspects in this case were multiplying like Harry's fleas. But why, I wondered, hadn't de France mentioned this one?

"You ought to go talk to him," said Burner.

"I'll do that," answered Barlowe.

"Any other questions?"

"Just one—where's the men's room?"

"I'll show you."

"Thanks," said Barlowe. "You're certainly very helpful."

Yeah, I thought, too helpful. As soon as Barlowe and Burner left, I padded over to the bookshelf. I told myself I was still taking it easy, letting Barlowe handle it, but that it wouldn't hurt for me just to check things out. I ran my nose over the books—a little trick I picked up from Harry—to find the one Burner had been reading. Then, I grabbed it with my teeth, pulled it out and shook it. The slip of paper Burner had stuffed inside fell to the ground. I looked at it. I could tell it was a drawing of some kind.

Then I heard footsteps. Quickly, I kicked the paper under the bookcase. The door opened. De France was standing there.

"Meester Bahrrrlowe, I'd like to see . . . Oh, it is only you. Ze dog."

I tried looking properly contrite in hopes that he'd accept my apology and leave so I could get that paper out from under

the bookcase. But de France didn't buy it. He glanced at the book I'd chucked aside. "Tsk, tsk. Naughty. Do not make ze mess," he said.

He picked up the book and read the title aloud. *"Ze Olde Alchemist's Guide to Herbs and Potions.* Well, *ma chienne,* you 'ave ze interesting taste, no? Now, where does zis go?" He found the place on the bookshelf and stuck the book back.

I thought maybe he'd leave then, but Barlowe walked in. "Find anything interesting, Sam . . . Oh, hello, Mr. de France."

" 'Ello, Meester Bahrrrlowe. I came to see 'ow you are doing. Is zere anyzing else you need or anyone else you care to interview?"

"No. Too bad about Amy Darling, though. I wanted to talk

with her. Paul Swete seemed pretty sad about her absence too."

"*Oui, l'amour.* For ze lover to be apart from 'is beloved is ze end of ze world."

Just as he said that, a tremendous explosion shook the room. And everything went black.

It took us a minute to realize what had happened. The explosion had knocked out the lights. But just for a moment. Soon, they blinked back on. The room and everyone in it was intact. But Barlowe and de France were all moving a little slow.

"Sam, are you okay?" asked Barlowe.

"*Wooff,*" I replied, meaning, Yeah, I still got all my body parts.

"What was that?"

"It came from ze lab," said de France.

I must've been as slow as everyone else because it took another minute for de France's words to register. Then they hit me. Hard. The lab! Roper! Roper was in the lab! With a howl, I jumped up and raced out the door.

CHAPTER
— 5 —

The lab door was open and people from all over the building were running toward it. Smoke was billowing out and the fumes made me choke. It smelled like someone had knocked over a vat of cheap cologne and added a couple of dozen rotten eggs to it for good measure. Paul Swete stumbled out. He sat down on the floor, coughing and rubbing his eyes.

"Stay away. There might be another explosion," someone warned.

"But there are more people in there," another voice said.

"Wait till the fire department gets here."

"The sprinkers probably took care of it . . ."

I didn't listen. I plunged right through the smoke. I ran past Paul Swete's and Bunson Burner's cubicles, past the communal lab. I couldn't see well because the fumes were making my eyes tear, but I kept moving. And all the time I was thinking if anything's happened to Roper because I didn't want to get involved in this case, I'll take myself to the pound. Permanently.

I stopped dead in front of the locked room that was to be the new chemist's. The door wasn't locked. In fact, it was hanging open by one hinge. I peered through the smoke and I could make out a desk, lying on its side with two of the legs broken off. Roper! I threw back my head and howled.

Then I heard a faint, sputtering voice say, "I'm here, Sam. Next door."

I turned and ran into Amy Darling's room.

"Under the desk, Sam," Roper gasped.

I stuck my head beneath and saw her curled up. I prodded her with my nose. She touched my head. She didn't seem hurt, just scared.

"Sam! Roper! Where are you?" Barlowe's voice rang out.

I gave a short bark. In a minute, he lurched into the room.

Roper crawled out, dusted herself off, and coughed. "I'm okay. It's a good thing de France put me in here. He said my room wasn't ready yet . . . That's where the explosion came from."

I let Barlowe see to Roper and slipped out. I had to check out the locked room. I knew it was risky, but it's a detective's job to take chances.

Carefully, I approached the doorway. The door was still hanging crazily and the desk was still on its side. Someone had turned on the fans and the fumes were being sucked out, so I could see (and breathe) better. What I saw was broken glass everywhere, mixed with what looked like a couple of chunks of plaster. There was a hole in the ceiling big enough for Santa Claus to squeeze through. And everything was covered with water—probably from those sprinklers someone mentioned. It was a mess. Sadie was going to have a lot of cleaning to do.

And then, right on cue, Sadie stood up from behind the overturned desk. She held a dustpan full of glass.

"Sam!" Barlowe's voice bellowed. "Where are you?"

Sadie looked up, startled, and saw me. She dumped the glass into the wastebasket and left in a hurry.

I watched her go and thought, de France is right. Sadie's sure efficient. In this case, too efficient. No one in her right mind would have risked her neck (and lungs) to clean up that room, no matter how efficient she was. It didn't make sense.

And something else didn't either. How did she get there so fast? Unless, I thought, unless she was already there.

But that was impossible. If Sadie had been in the room, she'd have been hurt. I looked around at the mess. Another thought hit me. Maybe Sadie had been hiding somewhere. There was a side door slightly ajar. I padded carefully over to it, stuck my head inside, and took a good whiff. Phew! I sneezed four times. Ammonia. Ammonia mixed with cheap perfume. No doubt about it. Sadie had been hiding in that closet when the explosion occurred.

The question was why?

The fire department got there fast. Three burly men checked out the room and told us there wasn't any danger of fire. At least not until "somebody conducts another experiment," the fire chief said to Roger de France, who was unsuccessfully trying to chew his moustache, which he couldn't reach because it was too thin.

"But nobody was conducting an experiment in ze new chemist's room," stated de France.

"Someone had to be," said the fire chief. "Explosions don't usually happen by themselves."

A faint gasp went up from the crowd hovering around the doorway of the lab. I scanned a couple of faces. Paul Swete was still recovering from the blast and the strange phone call. Bunson Burner looked scared. And Sadie was nowhere to be seen.

"We'll seal off the room and poke around to see if we can figure out what happened," said the fire chief.

I was glad to leave that investigation to the chief and his men. Walking around on broken glass is hard on my feet.

The crowd slowly dispersed except for Swete, Burner, and de France, who kept running his hands through his hair and babbling something about insurance. Barlowe turned to Roper and offered her a ride home since the lab was closed off and she was in no shape to work anyway. But Roper was recovering fast. "I'm all right, Mr. Barlowe. I'll check out the stock room. I've got to familiarize myself with the products here."

I could tell Barlowe was feeling guilty that he'd gotten her into this and he wanted her out of it as soon as possible. "But Roper, you don't know . . ." he began, almost blowing her cover.

Roper made a sound in her throat to cover up his mistake. "Thanks again, Mr. Barlowe. And I *do* know what I'm doing." She turned on her heel and walked away. It was the classiest exit I'd seen in a long time.

There was no need for us to stick around any longer, so we got into the Clunker and headed for Barry Slick's place. Barlowe had decided it was as good a time as any to interview Sol Ubal. Before we left, Barlowe had managed to ask de France why he hadn't mentioned Ubal as a suspect.

"Ubal?" de France had said. "Why he is so obvious. He went to work for Barry Slick. It is never ze obvious one, is it?"

Sheesh, as Barlowe would say, everybody thinks he's a detective.

During the ride to The House of Good Looks, the spaniel snoozed, not dreaming, and Barlowe didn't sing, so I had a little peace and quiet to think about questions like who had been working in the locked room? Why didn't anyone come forward to admit it? Sadie must've seen who it was, but why was she protecting him or her? Paul Swete was in the lab, so he had the opportunity. Bunson Burner had gone to show Barlowe where the men's room was. But he could've gone back to the lab . . . Bunson Burner! That paper! I never retrieved that blasted paper! The explosion and its aftermath had made me forget all about it. Sam, you're slipping, I berated myself. A good detective doesn't make any excuses for her failures. Well, it was too late to go back there. Maybe it would still be there the next day, I thought.

I stopped thinking about the paper and went back to thinking about suspects. Sadie, Swete, Burner. It had to be one of them. Or did it? Amy Darling had skipped town under suspicious circumstances. Had something or someone scared her? Maybe there was yet another suspect de France forgot to mention? Allison Keys? Not likely. What about de France himself? He was with us when the explosion took place, but the guilty party must have just left the experiment cooking and gone out or else he or she would have been blown up with it.

Slowly I scratched my ear. There were too many questions and not enough answers. I had the sinking feeling things were going to get worse before the end of the day.

And I was right.

CHAPTER
—6—

The House of Good Looks, Barry Slick's place, wasn't a Spanish hacienda. It was a French château (probably to make up for not having a French name). I know it was a French château because a couple of years ago Barlowe's cousin Fred went into the doghouse business. He figured he'd make a killing manufacturing doghouses that looked like rich people's fancy homes. He sent me one for Christmas—unassembled. Barlowe looked at the nuts and bolts and pieces of wood and began to read the instructions aloud: "How to assemble Fido's French Château." I hadn't heard the word before, but I understood what it meant. A château was something fancy, like a castle. We didn't have a backyard and I didn't need a doghouse, but Fred had sent a note along with the château saying he'd be dropping in on Christmas Day to see how I liked it.

It took Barlowe all night to put the thing together. It was half the size of our living room. He finished just as his cousin showed up. "Isn't it great?" boomed Fred.

"Great," Barlowe said through clenched teeth. He was exhausted.

"Go ahead in, Sam," said Fred.

Now, if it had been any other day, nothing could have made me crawl inside that thing, but it was Christmas and I was feeling charitable. I picked my way up the steps and walked inside. Château or not, it smelled like any doghouse does before it's been lived in. I sat down politely.

"She loves it!" Fred said excitedly. "Oh boy, I'm gonna be rich!"

That's when the thing collapsed. It didn't make a sound. It just fell apart. Fortunately, yours truly wasn't hurt.

After a moment of stunned silence, Barlowe's cousin said, "You must have done something wrong, Phil. How about trying it again?"

With a growl, Barlowe sprang at Fred and bounced him out the door.

We haven't seen him since. But this year, *Barlowe* got a present from him—a gizmo guaranteed to brush your teeth, comb your hair, and give you a shave, all at the same time. All you had to do was put it together. It's a good thing nobody was on the street below when Barlowe threw it out the window.

The House of Good Looks looked sturdier than Fred's doghouse and I didn't have any qualms about entering it. I noticed that, although it looked different on the outside from La Maison de Beauté, inside it was pretty much the same—from the layout right down to the receptionist whose face was covered with a goo that smelled suspiciously like de France's new skin cream. This time, I didn't make the mistake of getting too close to her. I didn't want to make a fool out of myself again.

"We'd like to see Mr. Slick," Barlowe told the receptionist.

"Do you have an appointment?" she asked in a nasal voice.

"No."

"Then I'm afraid you can't. Mr. Slick is a very busy man."

"So is Mr. Barlowe."

"Who's he?" asked the receptionist.

"I am. And I suggest you just pick up that phone and give

Mr. Slick a buzz to let him know I'm here." Barlowe was doing his tough guy act.

But the receptionist wasn't falling for it. "I told you, Mr. Slick will not see anyone without an appointment," she said, raising her voice.

"And I told *you* I don't have any time to waste," said Barlowe, raising his voice even louder.

While they were arguing, I slipped down the hall.

I didn't have any trouble finding Slick's office. It was in the same location as de France's in La Maison de Beauté. The door was closed, but I could hear Slick's voice on the other side. I didn't hear another voice, so I figured he was talking on the phone.

"You said he'd come through right away. That was three hours ago, and he still hasn't. Don't tell me to give him time. I want results, Ribsy. Results. I'm paying you enough for 'em."

Ribsy. The name rang a bell. But I couldn't place it.

"Okay, you've got till midnight. But that's all."

There was a silence, then I heard Slick say, "What is it, Miss Greason? Insists on seeing me? No appointment? Who? Barlowe? Barlowe! No, I don't want to see . . . Hmmm, on second thought, I think I will. Send him in."

I sat and waited outside the door until Barlowe showed up. He almost tripped over me. "Sam, how'd you get here?" he asked.

How do you think, I said to myself. Then I stood up and walked into Slick's office with him.

Barry Slick's office may have looked just like Roger de France's, but Slick himself didn't resemble his rival at all. He was big and burly, with a thick head of hair and a smile as wide as the state of Texas and just as oily.

"Well, Mr. Barlowe—and Sam Spayed. This is an *unexpected* pleasure."

I noticed he emphasized *unexpected* rather than pleasure.

"What can I do for you? I'm not in any need of a detective at the moment." Although I didn't think it would be possible, his smile got a little wider and a little oilier.

"That's okay, Mr. Slick. I've been hired . . . by Roger de France."

Well, Barlowe, I thought, it was very clever of you to let that slip. Very clever or very dumb.

"Oh, *Monsieur* de France," Slick said. "Is he complaining about me again? He always thinks we're stealing his products."

"Well, aren't you?" asked Barlowe.

"Mr. Barlowe, The House of Good Looks has its own group of talented, creative scientists. They come up with new and exciting ideas. If those ideas occasionally *overlap* with those of La Maison de Beauté, well, as de France himself would say, *c'est la vie*." He shrugged and waved his hand in a gesture of dismissal.

But he hadn't answered Barlowe's question.

"Well, Mr. Slick, I'd like to speak to one of those creative, talented scientists now."

"Oh? Which one?"

"Sol Ubal."

Slick's smile dried just a little and he hesitated for only a fraction of second, but it wasn't lost on me. Then, he turned on the oil pump once more. "Certainly. He's in the lab. Go on ahead. It's the last room on the left. I'll let him know you're coming."

What else will you let him know, I wondered. Slick didn't want to give us a chance to find out. He opened the door and ushered us both out. I trailed Barlowe a little way down the hall and then doubled back. I stuck my ear against the door and heard Slick say, "Barlowe's on the way to see you . . . Right. Plan A." I heard him hang up and start walking toward the door. I scuttled down the hall and caught up with Barlowe at the lab.

Sol Ubal, tall, lanky, and very calm, had just come out of the phone cubicle when we walked in. Barlowe introduced us. "I'll be happy to talk with you if you don't mind my tending to this stuff at the same time," said Ubal, crossing over to a pot cooking over a small burner. "Our new deodorant," he explained, stirring the mixture.

But it smelled like something else to me. Something all too familiar.

"Mr. Ubal, I'd like to ask you a few questions about La Maison de Beauté. You worked there until recently. Why did you leave?"

"I got a better offer here. Why else?" said Ubal.

Barlowe nodded. "While you were there, a couple of products ended up being stolen—by your new boss. Or rather by someone in his employ. What do you know about it?"

"Are you accusing me of *industrial espionage*, Mr. Barlowe?"

"I'm not accusing you of anything, Mr. Ubal."

Ubal let out a snort. "Listen, Mr. Barlowe, I'm going to tell you something. De France has been thinking people have been stealing his products for years. Frankly, I think he's a little funny up here." He tapped his head. "What's the word? *Paranoid.* That's it. I think de France is a little paranoid. The fact is, Mr. Barlowe, the chemists here are good. Very good. They don't need to steal from anybody. If The House of Good Looks beat La Maison de Beauté to the punch, it was just de France's hard luck. But hard luck isn't the same as industrial espionage."

This must be Plan A, I thought to myself, Ubal's parroting back exactly what his boss just said. I didn't need to hear any more of it. I had something more important to do, but I needed another minute or two so I wouldn't burn my tongue. Slowly, I began to edge toward the stove.

Ubal was still going on about de France's being a crackpot, but then his voice took on a different tone. He stopped sounding rehearsed and started sounding honest. "Still, wrong as de France is about the leaks, he may be right about something funny going on at the lab."

"What do you mean?" Barlowe asked. I had the same question.

"Well, I was walking by La Maison de Beauté last night around ten o'clock and there was a light on."

Barlowe didn't ask Ubal what he'd been doing there. Instead, he said, "A light?"

"Yes. In the lab. And I heard a strange sound coming from there too."

"What kind of sound?"

"A high-pitched sound. Like a dog yapping."

A mysterious yapping! Suddenly, I remembered the noise I had heard in the parking lot. Ubal had to be telling the truth.

"If I were you, I'd take a spin past there tonight about that time," Ubal said.

"Hmmm," said Barlowe.

I knew that the conversation was nearing an end. I had to act fast. *Bong!* I jumped up and knocked the pot off the stove and on to the floor.

"Sam!" Barlowe hollered.

What Ubal said is unprintable.

I managed a big slurp of the stuff he'd been cooking and leaped away just before his foot connected with my hindquarters. I hightailed it out of the room, with Barlowe close behind.

What I found out was worth my scorched tongue. Ubal had been lying. The "deodorant" tasted exactly like the goo on Miss Keys's face. Or, should I say, *almost* exactly. Something definitely was missing. Something that gave the goo—AKA Crème de Beauté—its extra pizzazz.

And then I knew for sure that no one had leaked Secret Formula 36 to Barry Slick and his outfit. Yet.

But I also knew it was only a matter of time before someone did. Unless I stopped the clock.

CHAPTER
—7—

Roper was already at our place when we got there. She'd let herself in with the key Barlowe once gave her. She explained that de France had decided to close up shop early and send everyone home so the fire department could do its job in peace.

I gave her the Big Greeting. I was glad to see her still in one piece. But after giving me a pat, she bent down to scratch the spaniel. So much for gratitude, I thought. I was about to head for my closet again, when Barlowe said, "I don't want you going back to that place, Mandy. It isn't safe."

The way he said it stopped me dead in my tracks. It stopped Roper too. Barlowe sounded worried. Really worried. It took both Roper and me a minute to recover. I sat down to listen. She stood up.

"I'm a big girl, Phil," she said. "I can take care of myself."

"You mean you won't quit?"

"No."

"Then, you're fired."

The way my head was switching back and forth, I felt like I was watching a game of catch.

"What do you mean—fired?" Roper shouted. "You can't fire me."

"Yes I can," said Barlowe. "I hired you."

"De France hired me."

Then Barlowe stopped me dead again—for the second time in five minutes. He grabbed Roper by the shoulders and shook her. "Will you listen to me for once?" he said.

I knew then he'd blown it. Roper stood up tall and stared him straight in the eyes. "No," she answered.

I would've applauded her if I could have. There's only one individual I know who's more stubborn than Roper once she decides to do something. Me.

Barlowe knew he was licked, but he tried to regain his cool. He let go of her, sat down in a chair, picked up the newspaper, and started to read it.

Roper sat down in the chair opposite his. "You want to hear my report?" she asked casually.

Barlowe kept right on reading. I wanted to tear the paper out of his hands, but I stopped doing things like that when I turned ten months old. Instead, I got up and sat next to Roper.

Finally, after a couple of minutes, he asked, "What report?"

"My report of what I found out today."

Barlowe didn't take his head out from behind the paper, but I heard a note of interest in his voice. "You found out something?"

"Yes," said Roper. "At least it might be something."

"What is it?"

"Well, I went into the library and Bunson Burner was there. He was scrabbling around on the floor on his hands and knees. I asked him if he'd dropped something. He said, 'No,' got up, and left in a hurry. I thought his behavior was a little odd, so I bent down and scrabbled around myself and I found this." She opened her purse and took out a slip of paper.

I recognized it immediately. It was the same paper with the drawing on it I'd kicked under the bookcase. Good work, Roper. You and I could make a good team, I thought. And if Barlowe keeps handling the case the way he has been, we may have to become one.

Barlowe put down his newspaper and held out his hand. "Let me see," he said.

Roper gave it to him. "What is this? It looks like a picture of a man with a lot of hair on his head."

"Never mind the drawing," said Roper. "Look at what's written on it."

Barlowe read the words aloud. " 'Secret Formula 36.' Secret Formula 36! And you think he was looking for this?"

"Uh-huh."

"Looks like we'll have to check out our friend Burner a little further." Then, grudgingly, he added, "Good work, Roper."

You're a little late with the compliments, I thought. But Roper just smiled at him and headed for the refrigerator.

I thought about the new piece of evidence. Something didn't fit, but I couldn't put my paw on it. I'd have to let it stew a little longer.

Roper came back with a container. She opened the lid and began to spoon something creamy into her mouth. My nose twitched as the smell drifted toward me. I walked over to Roper, my nostrils working overtime. I wasn't hungry, but that smell . . . I had to have a taste. Right away.

I went into the starving pooch bit. I let my tongue loll out and got that hangdog look. Roper laughed. "Here, Sam. Want some?" She held out a heaping spoonful. I gave it a big lick. And then I knew at once what the special ingredient in Secret Formula 36 was, the same ingredient missing from Ubal's concoction. It was yoghurt.

"*Bloof*," I barked.

The spaniel looked up. Her eyes were beginning to clear.

"You want some too, Beauty?" asked Roper.

I stared back at her. "Yoghurt"—the first word she'd said when I found her wandering in the middle of the street. Yoghurt. Then, "beauty"—that was the second word. And now she was about to say something else. What would it be? She opened her mouth. I cocked my ears. "Shipping crates," she said.

"Shipping crates?" I repeated.

"Shipping crates," she said once more, and then, as usual, her eyes went blank. But she took a lick of Roper's yoghurt.

"She's so ladylike," said Roper.

"Yeah. She's very polite," said Barlowe. "Wonder why her owner hasn't shown up. I put an ad in the paper. Maybe someone will respond to that."

I ignored them. My mind was racing.

Yoghurt. Beauty. Shipping crates. Three, no, four words that had nothing to do with each other. Or did they? I didn't know. But I had a funny feeling inside that I was overlooking something.

I tried instead to concentrate once again on the suspects in the case. Burner. Swete. Sadie. Ubal. Maybe even de France. Their faces flashed before me.

There's a pattern here somewhere, I thought, but right now it just looks like a bunch of dots to me. I had to figure out how to connect them to make a picture. I tried, but all I could see were the dots.

So I decided it was time to do something that never fails to help when I'm at a dead end. I decided to take a nap.

The nap was just what I needed. I didn't come up with any solutions to the case yet, but I felt rested and alert by the time Barlowe, the spaniel, and I walked into King's Bar that afternoon.

Barlowe plunked himself down at the counter, with the spaniel at his feet. I found myself a dark corner to wait in.

I didn't have to wait long. "So, how's the case going?" Harry asked in his rough voice.

"Not bad," I answered. "If you don't mind a few slivers of glass in your toes, a burned tongue, and an explosion or two."

"Sorry I asked."

"Never mind. It's all part of the job . . . So, tell me, what did you find out about 'Beauty' over there?"

For the first time since I've known him, Harry looked sheepish. "Uh, well, the truth is . . . nothing. I haven't found out a thing. I'm sorry, Sam. But nobody seems to know her. Either she's new in town or she doesn't hang out on the street much."

"I'll vote for the latter," I said. "She doesn't look like the kind who even knows what a lamppost is."

"Anyway, like I said, I'm sorry. But I'll keep trying."

"Thanks, Harry," I said, and meant it.

Our conversation was interrupted by the arrival of another customer, a skinny little guy with a pug nose who looked vaguely familiar. The spaniel took one look at him, yelped, and ran under the table next to me. I asked her if she was okay, but she didn't answer.

A fat guy came over to the skinny one. "Hey, Ribsy, when did you get out?" he asked.

Ribsy. My ears shot up.

"Hiya, Bulger. Last week," he said.

"Last week, huh? It's good to see ya. How about coming over for some poker tonight? The guys'd love to see ya."

"Not tonight, Bulger. I got me a . . . date."

A date! That was a code word if I ever heard one. I leaned in their direction. I didn't want to miss anything.

"A date?" said Bulger. "Where are ya going?"

"Uh . . . Loon Lake Park."

"Yeah? What time?"

"Uh . . . around eleven-thirty."

"A late date, huh? Need any extra company?"

"Nah, but my pal Quickdraw might."

"Well, how about giving me a call and letting me know."

"Okay."

"Good. You got my number. Hope to hear from ya." Bulger left.

Ribsy downed a quick drink and left too.

I turned to Harry. "Who are those guys?"

"Never saw the fat guy before, but I can tell a strong-arm man when I see one. The skinny one's named Ribsy. You've probably seen him here a few times a couple of years ago."

45

"Yeah, now that you mention it, I have. But who is he?"

"Small-time hood. Specializing in kidnapping and extortion."

"Kidnapping!"

"Yeah. Just got out of the Joint last week for stowing some creep's rich aunt in an abandoned Chinese laundry for a couple of days, so the creep could collect on her from his uncle."

"The creep get caught?" I asked, interested, even though it wasn't my case.

"Yeah."

I glanced over at the spaniel. She was snoozing calmly again. Weird dog, I thought. Then I turned back to Harry. "So, Ribsy's got a 'date' tonight. I wonder who the date is?"

Harry closed one eye and looked at me through the other. It's a habit of his. "Is it important?"

I gave him the same look he was giving me. "You might say so," I said.

Then I started to wonder how I was going to get Barlowe to get us to Loon Lake Park at 11:30 P.M. I had a feeling it wasn't going to be easy.

CHAPTER
— 8 —

It was 9:20. I knew that because the big grandfather clock in the living room was telling us it was 9:00. I hated the clock. It smelled musty and it was twenty minutes slow, as Roper always reminded us. But it was Barlowe's most prized possession because he'd won it. Not from one of those contests he always enters. No, he won it a couple of months ago in a raffle sponsored by the League of Retired Private Eyes. But he loved it just the same. The best thing I can say about the clock is that at least it doesn't say "Cuckoo."

Anyway, after the clock stopped striking, the phone rang. Barlowe waited for me to flip the speaker switch. I kept working on an itchy spot near my right ear, so he sighed and did it himself.

" 'Allo? Meester Bahrrrlowe?"

"*Oui* . . . I mean . . . yeah, this is Barlowe, Mr. de France."

"*Ah oui*. I 'ave some news. Ze fire chief, 'e say not to worry. Zat ze explosion it was caused by . . . er . . . spontaneous combustion. You know, when 'eat causes stuff just to go *poof*. I saw zat 'appen once in my grandmama's cellar in Paree. She kept some bottled gas—"

"Spontaneous combustion?" Barlowe cut in. "I thought the fire chief said someone was doing an experiment."

"Oh no, no, no," said de France quickly. "No experiment. Just spontaneous combustion. No need to check further."

"Hmmm," said Barlowe. I could tell he was thinking hard. So was I. What the Frenchman said didn't make sense. And the way he said it sounded even stranger. Like he was trying to cover up someone or something.

"Meester Bahrrrlowe, 'ave you any news for me?" de France put in before Barlowe could ask any questions. "About Crème de Beauté?"

"Is there anyone who works in your lab at night, Mr. de France?"

"At night? No, all ze chemists go 'ome by six. Why?"

"No reason," Barlowe said. I could tell he didn't want to unnerve de France. He decided to add his favorite soothing lines. "Sit back and relax, Mr. de France. I'm on top of the case."

They were about as soothing to de France as iodine is on a wound. " 'Ow can I sit back and relax wiz Barry Slick just waiting to steal my *crème*?" de France said, his voice rising.

"I'll see you tomorrow," Barlowe said hastily and hung up. He went back to working on a crossword puzzle.

But I kept thinking. Something was peculiar here. De France was protecting someone and yet he also sounded like he really wanted the leaks stopped and the spy caught. Was it possible the explosion and the "industrial espionage," as Ubal put it, had nothing to do with each other? I didn't have too long to wonder about it because the phone rang again.

Barlowe sighed. I knew he didn't want to hear any more from de France. "Yeah?" he said.

It wasn't de France. And it wasn't the same voice from the night before either. This one sounded like a 33 RPM record being played at the wrong speed. "If you want to solve your case, go to La Maison de Beauté tonight," the voice chirped.

"Who is this?" asked Barlowe.

"A friend," the voice said and hung up.

Barlowe sighed again. "Okay, Sam, let's go."

48

I didn't have to ask where. I knew. I only hoped we'd have time to make it to Loon Lake Park afterward.

The Clunker coughed a couple of times before it started. Then it took off slowly down the street.

My nose was itching worse than it had been the day before. But Barlowe didn't want to know about it. The only thing he was worried about was getting paid for this case, which he wouldn't be if he didn't come up with some hard evidence soon.

We made it to Garson Boulevard, minus the spaniel this time, and drove slowly past the lab. It was dark and quiet as a tomb. We rounded the corner. It was Barlowe's idea to park a block away so we wouldn't be spotted, then walk to La Maison and wait until someone showed up.

We parked and walked. But when we got there, the place wasn't dark anymore. There was a single light burning. And it looked to me like it was coming from the lab.

"Someone's in there," said Barlowe.

No kidding, I wanted to say, but instead, I walked to the door.

And then I heard the noise. It was just what Ubal had described. A high-pitched yapping. It was the same noise I'd heard in the parking lot that morning. Barlowe put his finger to his lips and opened the door with the key de France had given him. Then he pulled out a flashlight.

Trying to make as little noise as possible, we crept slowly down the hall. The yapping grew louder. We reached the lab and Barlowe flicked off the flashlight. He turned the doorknob slowly. The door opened with a little creak. The communal lab was bright as daylight, but the yapping had stopped. We entered and just had time to glance around at the test tubes and weird-looking vessels bubbling away when, *snap*, somebody shut off the lights.

"All right. We know you're there," said Barlowe, flicking on the flashlight once more and casting it around the room.

49

"Come out," he said.

There was no answer.

"I said, 'Come out.' "

Still nothing.

Then, I heard a noise to the left of me.

I stood still and listened until I heard it again. There. Behind the counter. I crouched low to the ground and moved toward it. I didn't need the light to tell me where to go. I just followed my ears and my nose.

Closer. Closer. Then I sprang. I grabbed hold of something bony. It was a wrist.

"Ouch! Let me go!" a man's voice shouted. He tried kicking me, and he got in a couple of good ones too, but I didn't let go.

Finally Barlowe found the wall switch. Light flooded the room. And there was Bunson Burner, his hand in my mouth, looking ready to cry. "Please let go of me," he whispered. "I won't run away."

I figured it was safe, so I released him. He slumped down, rubbing his wrist. "H-how d-did you f-find m-me out?" he murmured.

"Easy," said Barlowe. He held out the piece of paper Burner had dropped.

Burner took one look at it and this time, he did cry. So hard Barlowe couldn't get another word out of him.

"Take it easy, Burner. Just tell me if you already spilled the beans or when you were going to."

But Burner just kept crying. And in between his sobs he kept saying things like, "Fame. Glory. All gone. All gone."

It was getting embarrassing and therefore Barlowe was relaxing his guard. But I wasn't. I heard a noise coming from behind the desk. It was faint, but I could make it out. It was a single high-pitched yip.

I charged before Barlowe had time to blink. But even I wasn't prepared for what greeted me. It was a dog all right, one of the littlest I've ever met. But it didn't look like any breed I've ever seen—or any mixed breed either. His head was almost as bald as Bunson Burner's and his tail and legs

were hairless too. But his back was covered in patches with thick white bristles. All in all, he looked like someone had dressed him in a fur coat the moths had gotten at.

The dog was shivering and his eyes were rolling around in his head. I said loudly, "Hey, you okay?"

He opened his mouth. The voice was unmistakable. "I'm not a fighter. Please don't hurt me," he yapped.

"Can the noise."

He didn't.

I stuck my face into his. "I said, 'Can it.' Sam Spayed doesn't hurt anyone who's innocent. Now, buddy, just tell me your name and what's going on."

The dog stopped yapping. He looked at me and blinked. Then, in a calmer voice, he said, "Hey, I've heard of you."

"Yeah. I'm not surprised. Now, talk."

"My name is Pancho and I'm . . . uh . . . helping Mr. Burner with an experiment."

"*Mr.* Burner? Don't you live with him?"

"No. I live with a friend of his. I'm just staying with him temporarily."

"What kind of experiment are you helping Burner with?"

"I can't tell you. . . . It's a secret experiment. But it's not illegal or anything. It's for science," he said, proudly, trying to fluff out his moth-eaten coat.

And suddenly, the dots connected. Or at least some of them did. I stared at Pancho. "Let me just ask you one more question. What kind of dog are you?"

Pancho drew himself up—all five pounds of him. "I'm a Mexican hairless," he said.

That was all I needed to know. *The Olde Alchemist's Guide.* Burner's drawing of the man with a lot of hair. His fear of the new chemist. His nervousness at the fire department poking around. Now it all made sense. I knew what the secret experiment was. Burner was trying to create . . .

"A hair restorer?" Barlowe said.

I turned around to look at Burner. He was nodding and wiping his eyes.

Then I looked back at Pancho. His eyes were gleaming. "See, I told you it was a scientific experiment."

I wanted to laugh. This character thought I should be impressed. But as far as I was concerned, Pancho was living proof that science doesn't improve on nature.

Then, both of us went over to Burner and Barlowe.

"But what about this? Secret Formula 36," Barlowe said. "That's the same one in Crème de Beauté."

"Yes, well, I got this idea of adding our Secret Formula 36 to an ancient alchemical formula I found in a book. I was going to try that out next. You see, I've been working on this experiment for three years. I tested it on a number of animals— like Pancho here."

Next to me, Pancho puffed out his skinny chest.

"But as you can see, the mixture still has some kinks in it."

Barlowe took one look at Pancho and said, "I'll say."

Poor Pancho looked deflated. I guess he hadn't realized Burner didn't consider him one of his successes. He slunk away into a corner. I let him.

"I've been coming here a couple of nights a week and no one noticed before. But I guess someone finally did," Burner said.

"Yeah, someone did."

"Careless of me. You see, I wanted to keep it a secret until it was ready. Then, I'd reveal it to the world. 'Bunson Burner's Hair Restorer. Use it and you'll never be bald again.' You know how many men would give their eyeteeth to have hair like yours, Mr. Barlowe?"

Barlowe couldn't help it. He ran his hand through his thick hair and tried not to look smug.

"And now you've found me out. It'll get into the papers and someone will steal my work. . . ."

"Calm down, Mr. Burner. Nobody's going to tell anybody or steal your work. But I suggest after tonight you find a different place to perform your experiments."

"You'll keep it a secret, Mr. Barlowe?" Burner asked.

Barlowe nodded.

"Oh, thank you." He looked ready to kiss Barlowe's hand.

Barlowe backed away. "We'll leave you alone now."

"Thank you," Burner said again.

We left the lab.

"A hair restorer. Sheesh," Barlowe said as we marched down the hall. "For this I have to go traipsing around at ten-thirty at night."

Ten-thirty! That gave an hour to get to Loon Lake Park. More than enough time. How could I tip Barlowe off? Jump out the window when we get near the park? Too risky. Howl like crazy?

I was thinking hard as we walked out the door of La Maison de Beauté. I was still thinking when Barlowe turned to lock it. Suddenly, I heard a noise to my right. I whirled around.

"Now, Quickdraw," said a voice. I recognized it as Bulger's.

I heard a hiss like an aerosol can being sprayed. And then I was hit full in the face with a thick, mushy cloud that smelled like whipped cream. I was blind! I yelped and wiped frantically at my eyes.

Then I heard a *thump* and a *thud* and a couple of pairs of running feet. Barlowe! I wiped faster. I tried licking the stuff off. It *was* whipped cream. Hmmm, not bad, I thought, and kept licking. But I couldn't reach most of it. I stopped licking and took off after the feet. I could smell them, but I couldn't see a thing. I reeled and stumbled and fell into something large and soft. A bush. I rubbed my face against it. The whipped cream came off. I could finally see again. I spun around and ran after the thugs once more. But they were gone.

A chill went up my back. I ran to the doorway of La Maison de Beauté. What I saw made me throw back my head and howl. Sprawled across it, flat on his face, was Barlowe. And he wasn't moving.

CHAPTER
—9—

I went crazy. At least for a couple of minutes. I danced around Barlowe, poking, prodding, howling, licking. And still he didn't move. I was about to try some mouth-to-mouth resuscitation—which would have have been tricky for me to do—when he finally stirred and groaned. "Sam?" he moaned and tried to sit up. But he fell back with another groan. "Oh, my head! Those creeps got away, huh? I wonder who they were?"

I didn't need to wonder. I knew. Bulger and another thug named Quickdraw. Sent by Ribsy, who also made that last phone call telling us to go to La Maison de Beauté. I also knew who'd tipped him off. Sol Ubal, who'd handed us the story that got us here in the first place. But the story was true, and Ubal had seemed sincere. So, maybe Ubal told Barry Slick and it was he who got the bright idea to have Ribsy and his cronies put us out of commission. It didn't much matter who did what, though. The whole bunch was rotten, and I wasn't going to mind rounding them up at all. But first I had to get Barlowe out of there. Out of there and over to Loon Lake Park. And that wasn't going to be so simple.

Barlowe had managed to sit up, but he looked about as fit to drive as a prizefighter who'd just been down for the count. I helped him get to the Buick. He opened the door somehow and stumbled in. Then he looked at himself in the rear-view mirror. I could've told him that was a mistake. "Ugh," he said, taking in his matted hair and the dent in his scalp. He put the key in the ignition and then, like a punctured balloon, collapsed over the steering wheel. "Gotta rest," he muttered.

I was getting frantic. Loon Lake Park was too far to walk. And although I've got plenty of talents, driving a car isn't one of them.

Then I saw the headlights pull up behind us. Those goons were back to finish the job. I grabbed Barlowe's sleeve and shook it. He moaned. "Gotta rest," he said again and slipped down farther in the seat. I slipped down too. They weren't going to get me without a fight.

The window was open a crack and I could hear their footsteps approaching the car. Then, *tap, tap. Tap, tap.* Someone was rapping on Barlowe's window. From my position I couldn't tell who it was, but I got ready to attack when he opened the door.

I heard the squeak. Then a familiar voice said, "Phil? Oh no! Phil, you're hurt!" It was Roper.

I jumped up.

"Sam!" she cried.

I was so glad to see her I didn't even care that the spaniel was with her. And I didn't even wonder how they'd known to come here.

Roper told me anyway. "I went to your place and let myself in. I saw a scribble on your pad—'La Maison de Beauté, ten o'clock.' I had this funny feeling and decided to show up. It's a good thing I did." She was half-talking to herself and checking Barlowe for damage at the same time.

Roper and I managed to drag and shove Barlowe into the passenger's seat. She got into the driver's seat. The spaniel and I jumped in the back. I didn't mind her being there. As it turned out, she was about to do me a big service.

Roper turned the ignition key. The Buick began to cough. It sounded like its cold was turning to pneumonia. Clunker, don't fail us now, I prayed. The engine turned over and I sighed with relief. Roper eased the car away from the curb and took off as fast as it would go. We chugged down the road. Another five minutes or so and we'd be at Loon Lake Park. And I didn't know what to do. Barlowe needed a doctor—or at least a bed. But I needed to crack this case. Which was more important? My heart was pounding and my nose was so itchy I wanted to stick it in a bucket of calamine lotion, even though I knew it wouldn't cure the kind of itch I had.

The streets flew by. I saw the trees that marked the beginning of the park.

And then, the spaniel did a strange thing. She began to whine and scratch at the window like her life depended on it.

"Hey," said Roper, "down, sweetheart."

But the spaniel didn't listen.

She was so loud, Barlowe actually woke up. "Better walk her, Mandy," he said in a distinct voice. "She's gotta go."

"Phil, I've got to get you home first."

That's when I remembered the detective's creed: A cracked case is more important than a cracked head. Sorry, Barlowe, I thought, and joined in with the spaniel.

"Oh no, now it's both of them!"

"I'll be all right," Barlowe said. "Walk them. In the park."

Roper stopped the car and put the spaniel on the leash. She didn't bother with mine. The blonde was practically choking herself as she tugged on the leash. As soon as I got out of the car, I took off. "Sam!" Roper yelled. I headed for the lake as fast as I could. But I wasn't fast enough. When I got to the edge I saw through the darkness what looked like a rowboat in the middle of the lake. I could just make out two shadowy figures in it. It had to be Ribsy and his "date."

Sorry, Roper, I said to myself. Then, I plunged in.

Once away from shore, I moved my legs faster than the rowboat's oars could cut through the water. Faster *and* quieter. Ribsy and his date didn't hear me coming. But I could hear them. Ribsy's voice carried loud and clear over the water.

"Hand it over if you want to see your sweetheart alive and well again," he said.

Then Ribsy's "date" spoke. I recognized the voice right away. I was sorry I did. It was Paul Swete.

"How do I know you've really got her?" he said.

"This proof enough?" Ribsy gave him something.

Swete gasped and let out a sob.

"Okay? Now, hand it over."

The moonlight was bright enough for me to see Swete reach into his shirt pocket.

That's when, with a burst of speed, I shot forward, splashing and barking.

"What the . . ." yelled Ribsy, leaping up. "You? Bulger was supposed to put you and your pal out of commission." He swung his oar.

It whistled past my ear, missing me by inches.

"Watch out," shouted Swete.

Too late. The boat rocked and tilted and then turned over, sending both of them into the water. One was churning and splashing near me. I hoped it was Ribsy. I snapped at him, but all I got was a mouthful of water. It didn't taste too good. After this episode I'd probably need a double dose of penicillin, I thought. But I couldn't give up now. I put on some speed and saw Ribsy (I hoped) swimming the breaststroke just in front of me. My teeth were inches from his ankle when I heard Paul Swete gasp, "Help me! I can't swim."

I paused for an instant and Ribsy pulled ahead. I let him go. I couldn't let Paul Swete drown—even if he was the spy at La Maison de Beauté.

I reached Swete in a couple of seconds and grabbed his collar just as he was going under for the second time. But he was thrashing around so much he pulled free and went under again. "*Smooff!*" I ordered, meaning, Don't panic!

He didn't listen. I tried to get under him to buoy him up, but I couldn't even get near him.

I had to do something fast. I felt a bump against my side. It was the rowboat, bobbing upside down. In a flash I knew

what to do. If I could push the rowboat near enough to Swete for him to cling to, he'd be all right. I swam behind the boat and started to push. It wasn't easy, but I managed. I only hoped Swete wasn't unconscious and could reach the boat. I got to where I thought he was (I couldn't see with the boat in the way) and paddled quickly around the bow. Just in time to see Swete's hands clutch at the peeling wood. Whew, safe, I thought. But the relief didn't last long. Swete was too weak to flip the boat over, let alone row it. I had to get someone to do it for him.

And then I saw another boat heading our way. "*Bloof,*" I barked. I sounded feeble even to myself. But Roper heard me anyway. She was there in less than a minute. She pulled up alongside Swete and the two of us got him into her boat. Then, she helped me in. She wrapped her sweater around Swete and kept asking him if he were all right. He didn't answer.

When we got back to shore, Barlowe was waiting for us.

"What are you doing here? You shouldn't be walking around. You probably have a concussion," Roper was carrying on.

"I'm fine. I come from a long line of hardheads," said Barlowe.

You can say that again, I thought.

Then he noticed Swete. "You? What are you doing here?"

Swete was either in shock or in a fury because he didn't say a word.

"Leave him alone. He almost drowned," said Roper.

All this time nobody asked me how I was doing. I'd been attacked with whipped cream and almost beaned with an oar. I was practically numb from being in the water so long and I'd delivered Barlowe's culprit right to him. And did anybody care? I contemplated just taking off and leaving them all there to muddle through themselves when a bellow made me—all of us—spin around.

It came from the spaniel. Roper had tied her to a sapling for safekeeping. She was still tied to the tree. But the tree was no longer in the ground. Bellowing at the top of her lungs and dragging the tree, she was charging right at Paul Swete.

I started to run at her. Then I realized her bellows weren't cries of anger, but cries of joy. Tree and all, she leaped at Swete and managed to get her paws on his shoulders without strangling herself or killing him with the tree. Then she began kissing him madly.

"Jasmine!" Swete cried. "Oh, Jasmine! I was afraid I'd never see you again."

Roper and Barlowe blinked at each other. They were totally confused. But I wasn't. Suddenly, I knew just what was going on. Yoghurt. Beauty. Shipping crates. Jasmine. Paul Swete. La Maison de Beauté. It all fit. And it was even nastier than I'd thought.

CHAPTER
— 10 —

Barlowe was the first one to talk. "All right. What's going on here?" he said. Barlowe's always been a little slow. His getting conked on the head just added insult to injury (or vice versa).

Swete still wasn't talking so I decided to give him a nudge. Jasmine (Jasmine? Personally, I preferred Yoghurt) started to growl. I gave her a look that shut her up fast. Then, I stuck my nose in Swete's shirt pocket, pulled out a soggy envelope and dropped it in Barlowe's hand. I considered dropping it at his feet so he'd do at least a little work, but I didn't want him to get dizzy and pass out again.

He opened the envelope, took out an equally soggy slip of paper, and read, "Lano. Litho. Yoghurt . . . What is this?"

"Let me see that," said Roper. She took the dripping paper. "The ink's run. But I bet I can guess anyway. This is Secret Formula 36. Swete was about to hand it to the guy he was with—the one who got away—but Sam stopped him. Right, Sam?" She looked at me.

At last. Credit where credit's due. I wagged my tail—just a little—to let her know I appreciated it.

"But this dog, Jasmine—or whatever her name is—what does she have to do with the whole thing?"

Everyone turned to look at her and Swete. He sighed and

his lower lip trembled. "I might as well . . . talk. Jasmine is . . . Amy Darling's dog," he said, untying her from the tree.

"Amy Darling? Isn't she your girl friend? The one who looks like Roper here?"

Swete nodded. "So, you're a detective too," he said to her.

"Sort of," said Roper.

"But I thought Amy Darling's out of town with her sick mother," said Barlowe. "What was her dog doing running around in the streets?"

Swete let out a sob. "Amy's not with her sick mother. Amy's been . . . kidnapped."

Right on cue, Jasmine started to howl.

"Kidnapped? What for?"

I nearly started to howl myself. Come on, Barlowe, you can do it. Even with that dent in your skull you can figure out what happened.

But it was Roper who answered. "You mean Slick and his outfit had her kidnapped and held for ransom to force *you* to give them the formula. But why didn't they get the formula from her?"

"We all worked on the formula," Swete said brokenly, "but only I knew the exact proportions. Slick's outfit faked Amy's call to Allison Keys, or forced her to make it. Then they called me yesterday when you were in my office. That's why I was acting so strange."

"But what about the dog?"

Jasmine was still howling. Now, I respect sentiment as much as the next canine, but enough is enough. "Shut up," I told her.

"They must've tried to kidnap her too. Jasmine and Amy are very close. But somehow, she got away," said Swete. "Now, I've got to find Amy before it's too late. . . ."

"What do you mean, 'too late'?"

"Don't you see, Mr. Barlowe?" Swete tried to stand up, but his knees were still too weak from his ordeal, so he had to sit down again. "You caught me before I could give them the formula. Now they have no reason not to hurt Amy. I've got to find her and stop them. . . ." He grabbed the spaniel. "Jasmine, where's Amy? Where'd they take her?"

Exactly what I wanted to know myself.

But Jasmine was still hysterical. So I did the only thing I could. I bit her.

"*Owww*," she yelped. But she stopped howling.

"Listen, you've got your memory back now, so if you want to see Amy Darling again, you better talk and talk fast," I said.

"I . . . I don't have it all back. They hit me. On the head."

I felt a little more sympathetic. I hadn't realized she'd been boffed. I just thought she was the hysterical type who lost her memory out of fear. So I said more gently, "You said four words while you were amnesiac: one, *yoghurt*, which, as it's the special ingredient of Secret Formula 36, you must've heard Amy talking about; two, *beauty*, for the products of La Maison de *Beauté*; and three, *shipping crates*, which you said right after you mistakenly recognized Roper as Amy . . . that's it!"

"What is?"

"Shipping crates! You said, 'Shipping crates.' Listen kid, does *warehouse* ring any bells?"

"Warehouse?" All of a sudden, Jasmine's eyes went funny again.

I got ready to bite her a second time, but it turned out I didn't have to. Her eyes focused and, in a strong, clear voice, she said, "Quick! We have no time to lose." Then, she ran out of the park.

I ran after her. We made it to the Clunker in record time and whined and scratched at the door so Barlowe, Swete, and Roper wouldn't fail to get the message when they caught up with us.

They finally did and Barlowe opened the doors. Jasmine and I jumped in, keeping up the whining.

"I think they know something," said Swete.

Barlowe didn't reply. But, claiming he was now fit to drive, he started the car.

"Which way?" I asked Jasmine.

"Straight, then turn right."

We pulled out, heading straight.

"Do you know where we're headed, Barlowe?" asked Roper.

"I'm following my nose," he answered.

"Here's my turn," said Jasmine. "How do we let them know?"

"Hurry," said Paul Swete to Barlowe.

I was thinking fast. "Know how a pointer works?" I asked Jasmine.

"Yes."

"Good. Then follow me." Making my head and right paw straight as an arrow, I stuck them out the right window and yelled, "*Clooff*," meaning, Turn right. Jasmine did the same.

"Hey, you just went out," Barlowe said to me.

"*CLOOFF!*" we repeated.

"I think they know something," Swete said again.

Barlowe was almost past the turnoff.

"They're pointing," said Roper. "They're pointing . . . right! Turn right."

She yelled so loud that Barlowe let go of the steering wheel. The tires squealed. The Clunker spun wide and almost hit a lamppost. Barlowe grabbed the wheel back, steadied the car, and made the turn.

"A left next," said Jasmine.

We repeated the procedure, using the left window and our left front paws. Roper watched us and navigated. "Turn left," she told Barlowe.

We're going to make it, I thought.

The Clunker chose that moment to die.

Barlowe turned the key. Nothing.

Jasmine began to whine and scratch the upholstery. "Cut it out," I said. Her whine changed to a howl.

He tried again. "I think it's the carburetor," he said.

"More likely the gas pump," said Roper.

"Who cares what it is. We've got to get Amy!" Swete yelled.

Barlowe swore and turned the key once more. No use. The Clunker had given up the ghost for real this time. Barlowe tore open the door, jumped out, and flung up the hood.

That was Jasmine's last straw. With a cry, she leaped out the open window and started running down the street.

There was nothing I could do but follow.

"Hey!" Barlowe called, but I didn't stop.

I had a heck of time keeping up with her. She was fast. Really fast. But then again she hadn't just spent the evening doing laps in Loon Lake. I could hear Barlowe, Roper, and Swete clattering somewhere behind us. But I knew they weren't going to be able to catch up.

"Slow down," I yelled, panting. "We're losing them."

But Jasmine wasn't listening. She raced into the street.

"Watch out!" I cried.

A car slammed on its brakes, missing her by inches. But she didn't pay any attention. She was determined to save her friend Amy. Even if she got herself wiped out in the process.

She made it to the sidewalk again and turned a corner on what looked like two legs.

I knew we'd lost the others for sure now. So there was nothing I could do but keep following her. On and on we ran, through the shadowy streets, with me always a few yards behind. After a while, the houses, buildings, cars, trees, melted away. Even the lights faded. There was just Jasmine and me, running, running. I felt like I was in some kind of dream.

We rounded another corner. And then, Jasmine stopped under a streetlight so fast I plowed into her.

I had to catch my breath before I could see where we were. It was a deserted street in front of a big, black building that had to be none other than the warehouse of The House of Good Looks. And in front of the big black building was a big black car from which two figures were emerging.

I grabbed Jasmine by the collar and jerked her back into the darkness. "Don't talk," I commanded. "Not one bark."

She took my advice.

"So, we take her for a ride?" said one of the figures.

"Yeah. A long ride. We'll just give her time to put on her shoes—her *concrete* shoes—before taking a swim in the lake," said the other.

I recognized his voice. It was Ribsy. I'd never seen or heard the other guy before. For them to have gotten to the warehouse so fast, he must have been waiting for him near the park.

The two men laughed. Then, the other one asked, "How will we get rid of that Swete character? He knows you. He could testify . . ."

"Don't worry. Ribsy always finds a way."

"Not the last time you didn't. You ended up in the Joint

when—" The rest of his sentence ended in a squeal.

"Care to repeat that, Crusher?"

Crusher didn't answer. Then he and Ribsy disappeared into the building.

Jasmine was shaking from head to tail. "It's them. . . . They've got her in there. I've got to save her. They're going to—"

I cut her off. "What are you planning to do? Charge the front door and go for their throats? You wouldn't make it past their knees. Those guys are armed and dangerous. If we're going to tackle them, we need a plan of action."

Jasmine calmed down. "All right. What's our plan?" she asked.

The plan was a little hazy in my mind. Step one had to be getting into the warehouse somehow. "First we check out the building," I said.

Hugging the wall, we circled the place. The windows were too high for us to reach. The doors were all locked. And Jasmine was starting to get hysterical once more.

"I've got to get in," she said, her voice beginning to rise.

And then I saw it. A head-high dull glint of metal set in one wall. A grate. I pushed against it and it swung in, leaving just enough room for a couple of dogs to slip through one at a time.

"Come on," I whispered.

I went first. Jasmine followed.

It was pitch-black inside. I couldn't see a thing. But I could smell well enough. I sniffed the air. "What is that?"

"Bath oil," said Jasmine, picking out a faint scent. "There're barrels of bath oil here. One's a little leaky."

I didn't bother to ask her how she knew it was bath oil. I figured she had enough experience in that category.

"Where do you think they are?" Jasmine asked. She was playing follow the leader now, with me in control. I didn't want to let her down, but the truth is, I didn't know what to say.

Then Ribsy's voice rang out, "Untie her feet, Crusher.

Don't try anything funny, girlie. This ain't a water pistol."

"They're next door!" Jasmine gasped. "What do we do now?"

I paused, waiting for inspiration to strike.

Suddenly, from somewhere in the darkness, a low voice said, "If I were you, I'd create a diversion."

Jasmine yelped and jumped twenty feet into the air. I stayed on the ground. Like I said before, it takes a lot to surprise me.

I turned toward the direction of the voice. "I think you're right on target, Harry," I said. "Right on target. We do need to create a diversion, and I know just how to do it."

CHAPTER
— 11 —

I didn't waste time asking Harry what he was doing in the warehouse. I didn't have any time to waste. Besides, Harry works in ways that are mysterious even to me.

I explained my idea quickly just as Ribsy's voice called, "Okay, move it, girlie."

"Ready?" I whispered.

"Yes," said Jasmine, planting herself where I told her to. She was one determined dog. And I respected her for it.

"Yeah," said Harry.

"Okay, go!" I barked.

Harry and I dashed around the room, knocking over crates, barrels, boxes, making as much noise as we possibly could. Then we stopped—just in time to hear Ribsy holler, "What was that?"

"I don't know. Sounds like it came from next door," said Crusher.

"We better have a look," Ribsy told him.

I hunched down, hoping Harry and Jasmine were doing the same. The door swung open and two flashlights beamed into the room. I could just make out two men. Crusher had a flashlight and a gun. Ribsy was holding Amy Darling and he had his hands full, trying to jockey her, his gun, and his flashlight.

"Whew, what a mess!" said Crusher. "You think it was rats?"

Ribsy ignored him. "Who's there?" he demanded sharply. None of us said a thing.

"All right, come out reaching for the peaches," Ribsy said. "I've got the girl here and the piece I'm holding against her head ain't no apple pie."

Yeah, and this ain't no fruit salad either, I wanted to tell him. But I didn't.

"Maybe we should turn on the lights?" Crusher said.

"Maybe I should have brought Bulger or Quickdraw with me instead of you," snapped Ribsy.

"I thought you said they messed up with that dog and that's how you landed in the lake."

"Forget them and forget the mutt too. She ain't here now. Just find those lights."

Crusher took a few steps forward. Suddenly, something dark and round rolled out across the floor toward him.

Blam! Blam! Shots rang out from Ribsy's and Crusher's guns. Then, just as we'd planned, Jasmine and I leaped out and grabbed Ribsy's and Crusher's ankles. Crusher screamed. His gun and flashlight clattered to the floor. Ribsy's flashlight went too, but I didn't hear his gun drop. What I did hear was Amy Darling's footsteps bolting through the door, followed by Jasmine's.

"The girl got away! After her!" Ribsy shouted.

Crusher answered with a moan. "Rabies! I'm gonna get rabies!"

I didn't bother to tell him I'd had my shots. I just leaped on him and down we both went, slipping and sliding in the bath oil pouring from the barrel he and Ribsy had put a few bullet holes in. Harry came tearing out with a growl to tackle Ribsy. I heard them crash to the floor too. We were wrestling dog-style, which is the same as wrestling regular-style—except in dog-style, you can use your teeth.

I landed a good nip on Crusher's calf, then jumped up. I was a few feet from the grate and could make it in one easy jump.

I called to Harry, "Go for the grate. Jasmine and Amy must be gone by now. Hurry!"

"I can't. He's got my ear," Harry rasped back.

If there's one thing I don't do, it's leave a friend in the lurch. I took a flying leap and landed on Ribsy's back. He was still soggy from the lake and I would've laughed if I hadn't had to hang on so tight.

It took Crusher a moment to realize he was free of his attacker. But even with the delay, he got the edge. He scrambled to his feet. His hand brushed the wall and found the light switch. At least, that must've been how it happened because suddenly the room was ablaze. "Look out, Ribsy!" he shouted, which Ribsy, with Harry and me on top of him, couldn't do. Harry and I turned toward Crusher, but it was too late. Crusher was pointing a long nozzle in my direction. And the next thing I knew, eighty-five pounds of water pressure knocked me on my back.

I was choking, gasping, begging him to stop. So was Harry. But Crusher went on spraying the firehose at us. I was going to drown. I knew it for sure. But not in water. In . . . bubbles.

The water had mixed with the bath oil, and now bubbles were rising around me and Harry like a tidal wave. Higher and higher. Up to our chests. Our necks. Our noses. "Help!" I tried to howl and got a mouthful of bubbles. I don't know how Ribsy managed to escape them, but he did. I could hear him laughing an evil laugh, somewhere across the sea of bubbles.

I thanked Harry for being the best operative a detective could have, Roper for being a good pal, and Barlowe for being lots of things too sentimental to mention. The last thing I said to myself was, Bye, Mom, wherever you are. Then, the bubbles went over my head.

Suddenly, a hand pulled me out of the sea and held me in a viselike grip. "Got 'em both," Crusher's voice said. I could tell how he got his name. I coughed and sputtered and wiped at my eyes. When they cleared, I could see Ribsy holding a gun on me. "So, it is you," he said. "You just ruined my career for me. You helped that girl get away. Too bad I couldn't finish

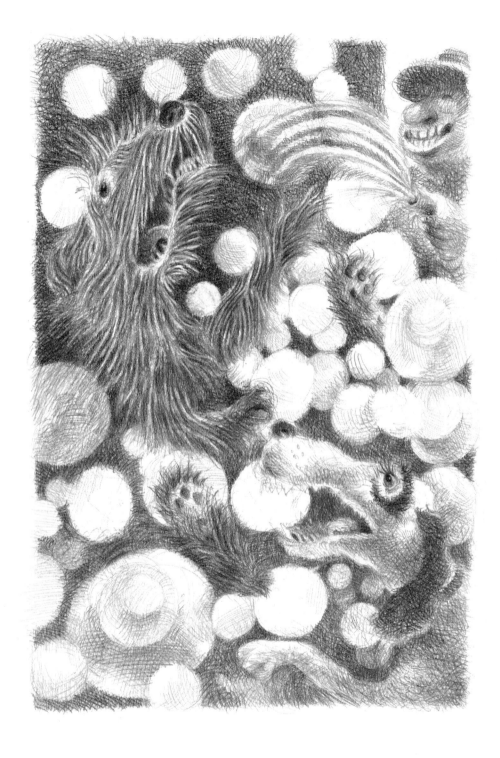

the job on you in the lake. But I will this time. On you *and* your pal. Take 'em outside, Crusher. We don't want to dirty Mr. Slick's nice floor here, especially after we just washed it so clean."

It's hard to think straight and fast when someone's holding a gun to your head. But that's what I had to do. Once Crusher and Ribsy got us out of here, they could dispose of us where nobody would ever find us. Unless we could get away. I tried wriggling a little. But Crusher's grip wouldn't quit.

And then I had an idea. I figured it might work. And besides, I had nothing to lose. I closed my eyes, opened my mouth, and howled. "Sing along with me, Harry," I warbled.

Harry caught my drift and joined in.

"Shut up!" Ribsy shouted.

Up an octave. Harry and I were hitting notes we didn't know were there.

"Stop them!" Crusher screamed. "Make them stop!" He seemed to forget he was the one who could do that. And was his grip loosening just a little?

I strained to high C and beyond. Any higher and my vocal cords would snap.

And then, a third voice chimed in. It was sharp and nasty, but both Harry and I thought it was the most beautiful voice we'd ever heard. It was the warehouse's alarm siren and it was singing with us in perfect three-part harmony.

"Ee-ahh!" Crusher yelped, as he dropped us.

But Ribsy held fast. He was vibrating from head to toe, but he didn't drop his gun. "Don't run or I'll shoot you right now," he said.

I stared at the muzzle and thought, I should've taken it nice and easy and let Barlowe solve this case, like I said I was going to. Well, it's been a good life, most of the time.

And then above the din, a voice rang out loud and clear. "I wouldn't if I were you," it said.

Ribsy whirled around. So did I.

There, in the doorway, was Barlowe, holding a .38.

For once, I thought his timing was pretty good.

CHAPTER
— 12 —

Just as we escorted Ribsy and Crusher out of the warehouse through the front door (the lock of which Barlowe had shattered with the .38), Roper rushed up and hugged me. "Oh Sam, I'm so glad you're all right." It was so swell to have her acting that way again, I forgave her for going gaga over Jasmine. "Barlowe finally got the car started and we drove around and around. We didn't know where to go," she continued. "If we hadn't seen Jasmine and Amy running through the streets, I don't know what would've happened."

I did, and I preferred not to think about it.

Where are Jasmine and Amy? I wondered. I turned my head. Amy was in Paul Swete's arms and Jasmine was dancing circles around them. I was glad they were all reunited, but I thought they might show a little more appreciation for Harry and me. Speaking of Harry, I turned my head in the other direction to thank him, but he was gone. Maybe it was just as well too, because there wasn't any way to thank him enough. Except to produce a couple of thick, juicy porterhouse steaks I didn't have.

Then the cops arrived, summoned by the siren still blasting away in the warehouse.

A familiar cop got out of the car and came over to us.

"Hello, Barlowe, Sam," said none other than Inspector Peevers. It figured that the cop who showed up was the one both Barlowe and I voted Last Person in the World We'd Like to Be Stranded on a Desert Island With. "Long time, no see," said Peevers.

Not long enough, I thought. Barlowe just grunted.

"Good work, Phil. This pair won't be getting out of jail so fast this time," Peevers went on.

Phil! Peevers never called Barlowe by his first name. And he certainly never praised him. I wondered what Peevers was up to. I didn't have to wait long to find out.

"Uh . . . Phil . . . I . . . uh . . . I've got . . . uh . . . a favor to . . . uh . . . ask you," he said.

"Yeah? What is it?" asked Barlowe.

"Uh . . . well, the mayor's going to appoint a new police commissioner, you see, and if he . . . could be made to . . . uh . . . believe . . . I got here before you did . . . it sure would help."

Barlowe was a little slow on the uptake. "But you *didn't* get here before I did," he said.

Peevers smiled like he was auditioning for a toothpaste ad. "Well, Phil, I know that, but if the mayor *thinks* I did . . ."

"Why would he think that?"

I could tell Peevers was starting to get irritated, but he was also trying not to show it. His smile became even broader. "Well, because I . . . uh . . . I'd tell him I did."

Barlowe furrowed his brow. "Why would you do that?"

Peevers's smile stretched so far I thought his mouth would snap like a rubber band. "Because then I'd get the job."

"Oh, I get it," said Barlowe.

"Good, good," said Peevers. He actually patted Barlowe on the back.

Then, a short, dark man rushed up to Barlowe. "Squib, from the *Daily Daily*. Is it true you just captured these two kidnappers single-handedly?"

Barlowe turned to the reporter and said, "Well, I wouldn't say single-handedly. It was me and . . ." He paused.

Peevers kept smiling—and waiting.

"And?" asked Squib.

"And Mandy Roper."

Peevers stopped smiling. I knew how he felt.

Barlowe wasn't the only one who let me down. In the *Daily Daily* story, the only place I appeared was in the photo. And that was blurry. That'll teach me to help Barlowe out, I thought. Next time I won't even go along as bodyguard. I'll just stay in bed. Or maybe I'll take a holiday with Roper and keep her out of trouble.

Even de France wasn't giving me credit. He threw a party two weeks after the case closed at La Maison de Beauté in *Barlowe's* honor. But at least he had the sense to serve some little chicken liver and bacon things along with the punch and potato chips. True, the liver was cooked instead of raw, but still, it showed some forethought on his part.

So that's where we were all gathered—me, Barlowe, Roper (who'd revealed her true identity to the assembled), de France, Swete, Amy Darling and Jasmine, Bunson Burner (who kept winking at us as if to say, "We've got a secret, don't we?"), and even Allison Keys (whose hair was standing up in stiff peaks all over her head, smelling like someone had poured one of Rex King's beer kegs over it). But someone was missing. De France was telling us about the newly renovated lab room where the explosion had occurred. "Looks as good as new," he was saying when I realized who was missing. I edged toward the door, but stopped because de France had clapped his hands. "Everybody, *écoutez*, listen. I 'ope you are enjoying zis party. As you all know, it is in honor of Philippe Bahrrrlowe. Because of 'im, Barry Slick and Sol Ubal are now in jail, along wiz Ribsy, Crusher, and two more men named Bulgar and Queeckdraw. Ubal was ze one who leaked ze information ze last two times when he was working 'ere, which is strange because he is too obvious a suspect . . ."

I wanted to laugh. De France was still playing detective. But I didn't bother to because it was about then in his speech that my nose started itching. Oh no, not trouble again, I thought, and tried to move to the door once more, but Bunson Burner and Allison Keys were blocking it.

"But Ubal got scared of getting caught," de France continued, "and so Slick 'ired 'im. Zey boz decided to set up Paul Swete. But zey went too far zis time. Zose crooks got involved wiz even nastier crooks . . ."

I tried scratching my nose, but it didn't work. I had to get out of the room. Images were coming to me. Images of Sadie looking through the garbage. Sadie smelling first like ammonia, then like ammonia mixed with cheap perfume. Sadie cleaning up broken glass in the lab. Sadie hiding in the closet. And suddenly, I knew where she was and who she'd been protecting. I began to scratch at the door.

"And so zey got caught. And it is Philippe Bahrrrlowe who caught zem."

Applause and cries of "Hip hip hooray for Barlowe!" This time, I didn't even bother to get annoyed that they weren't cheering for me. I scratched harder. Then I poked Allison Keys's leg. She looked down and smiled. "Want to go outside, honey?" she asked.

I scratched at the door again and she opened it. I streaked down the hall as fast as I could until I got to the lab. The lab door flew open and out flew Sadie, reeking of a different, but equally cheap-smelling, perfume. She threw herself on the floor. I didn't bother to ask why. I joined her. Just in time. If we hadn't already been lying down, the explosion in the lab would have knocked us down for sure.

I was still holding on to Sadie's dress when Barlowe and everyone else showed up. I wasn't holding on too hard. I didn't have to. Sadie was as immobile as a car with four flat tires.

"Okay, spill it," said Barlowe. "What's going on here?"

Sadie glanced up wearily at de France, who seemed to have gone several shades paler. Then she looked back at Barlowe. "Why don't you ask Mr. de France? He can tell you," she said.

Everybody looked at de France.

"Okay. What's going on here?" Barlowe said again.

I didn't tell him he was repeating himself. I was waiting to find out if what de France had to say matched with what I suspected.

"Well, I believe Sadie 'ere 'as been doing a little experimenting on 'er own. I believe she 'as been trying to reproduce Soft Shoulders *parfum*. She apparently searched ze . . . er . . . garbage . . . for clues 'ow to make it. I believe she also tried to put you off ze scent, Meester Bahrrrlowe, by calling you one night. She did not want her work disturbed."

So it was Sadie who made that first call. I should've guessed.

"Soft Shoulders! That's one of the most expensive perfumes around!" said Paul Swete.

"And we don't even make it. Trop Cher does," said Amy Darling.

"I know," said de France. "But recently, Bunson made a test batch of a very similar and cheaper *parfum*. You said it needed work and tossed it and ze formula away. Remember?"

"Yes," said Burner.

"Sadie figured if she could reproduce zat batch she could sell it at a lower price on 'er own."

"When did you find this out?" asked Amy.

"Er . . . after ze explosion."

"You mean you found out weeks ago that Sadie not only was trying to rip off Trop Cher just like The House of Good Looks was doing to you, but she also almost blew up the building, and you didn't try to stop her?" Amy said.

De France lowered his eyes.

"Well, why didn't you?" asked Roper.

"Might as well tell them, Bernie," said Sadie.

"Bernie?" said Barlowe.

Roger de France nodded slowly and in perfect Brooklynese said, "Yeah, Bernie. Bernie Schwartz from Borough Park. Bernie Schwartz who's never been to Paris in his life. Bernie Schwartz—at your service." He bowed mockingly.

Everyone looked surprised. Everyone except me. I always thought his accent sounded phoney.

Then the former Roger de France took Sadie's hand and helped her to her feet. "And now I'd like to introduce you all to Sadie Schwartz. My dear, sweet mother."

For a long minute, no one said a word. Then Sadie's voice cut through the silence. "Okay," she said. "Everybody out of here. I've got work to do."

We all went. And nobody dared to laugh until we were well out of Sadie's hearing range. After all, she was still twice the size of any of us.

"Well, I don't know about you," said Roper as Barlowe unlocked the door to our place, "but I don't ever want to see or smell perfume, skin cream, or anything made by La Maison de Beauté, The House of Good Looks, or Sadie Schwartz ever again. Or at least not for a very long time."

I knew exactly how she felt, although there had been a couple of smells I wouldn't mind sniffing again.

Barlowe didn't answer. He set our mail down on the coffee table. Then slowly he turned to Roper. "I . . . uh . . . I didn't thank you for the . . . uh . . . work you did on the case," he said, stumbling over his words.

You didn't thank me either, I thought, but I kept my mouth shut because Barlowe's thanking anybody was a big improvement.

"Well, thanks," said Roper, her face lighting up.

"Next time you . . . uh . . . go on vacation maybe Sam and I'll . . . uh . . . come along."

There goes my holiday, I thought. But I had to hand it to Barlowe. This was more than an improvement. This was a personality change.

Roper was smart enough not to make a big thing out of it. She just nodded. Then, before the silence got too uncomfortable, she said, "So, Barlowe, aren't you going to open your mail?"

He smiled and sorted through the envelopes. One slid to the floor. I trotted over, picked it up, and handed it to him. It smelled familiar. Too familiar.

"Hey, look at this! It says 'Eggelant' on the envelope."

"Eggelant? Isn't that a shampoo? And didn't they just sponsor some big contest or other?" said Roper.

"Yeah. I entered it. Maybe I won."

"Well, hurry up and open the envelope," said Roper.

I began to get a funny feeling in my stomach, but I wasn't sure whether it had to do with the scented letter or the extra-large porterhouse steak I'd eaten that morning.

Barlowe ripped open the flap and pulled out a single sheet of paper. " 'Dear Mr. Barlowe, Congratulations! Your slogan has won you a prize in the Eggelant (Egg-Rich) Shampoo contest . . .' Hey, I did it! I won! Yippee!"

He threw the envelope, the letter, the rest of the mail, in the air and began to jump around the room like a five-year-old kid. The only problem is that Barlowe is thirty-six.

Roper bent down and picked up the letter. "It says a messenger will deliver your prize on Thursday, June 20 . . . Barlowe, that's today!"

Barlowe didn't stop jumping around. "Today! Whoopee! I'm gonna be rich!"

I thought it was a good thing none of our clients was watching. I wished I weren't either.

"It doesn't say what the prize is, though," said Roper.

Barlowe either didn't hear her or he didn't want to.

But we all heard the buzzer when it sounded. Barlowe danced over to the intercom. "Who is it?" he sang.

"Messenger from Eggelant Shampoo."

"Come on up." Barlowe grabbed Roper and started to cha-cha with her across the room.

I was glad our elevator is a fast one. The messenger was at our door in no time.

Barlowe flung it open. "Come in, come in."

For a moment I was afraid he was going to hug the figure in uniform, but he didn't.

"Sign here, please," said the messenger.

Barlowe did.

Then the messenger stooped and picked a big box off the floor. "Here you are. Congratulations." He left quickly.

We all stared at the box and Barlowe's face fell. I knew we were all thinking the same thing. If that box was full of money, our names were Lad, Lassie, and Rin Tin Tin.

Roper tried to be delicate. "Well, maybe you won the second prize," she said.

Barlowe brightened a little. "Yeah. Maybe."

"So, open it already," said Roper.

Barlowe got a knife and cut through the tape. He pried away the lid and pulled out mounds of straw packing. "Here it is!" he announced, up to his elbows in the box. Carefully, he lifted something out. In one hand was a slip of paper, in the other, a couple of jars. He read the paper aloud. " 'From the people who bring you Eggelant.' " Without looking at its label, he unscrewed one of the jars. The familiar aroma wafted across the room. I couldn't mistake it even if I tried. It was Crème de Beauté. A whole case full.

It took Barlowe and Roper a little longer to realize what he had won. When they did, they both had to bite their lips— Roper to keep from laughing and Barlowe to keep from crying.

As for me, I didn't have to keep from doing either. When you're a detective, you know those are the breaks.

Besides, I'm the thrifty type. I figure when we get broke and hungry enough—which will probably be in the not too distant future—the stuff will come in handy. It may not be porterhouse, but that face cream is still pretty darn tasty.